If Wishes Were Horses

Virginia Vail

If Wishes Were Horses

Produced by Alloy/17th Street Productions, 151 West 26th Street, New York, New York 10001.

Original title: If Wishes Were Horses
Cover illustration: © Paul Casale/1994 Daniel Weiss Associates, Inc.
Cover layout: Stabenfeldt A/S
Typeset by Roberta L. Melzl
Editor: Bobbie Chase
Printed in Germany, 2007
ISBN: 1-933343-53-2

Stabenfeldt, Inc.
457 North Main Street
Danbury, CT 06811
www.pony.us

ONE

IN THE PALE LIGHT OF EARLY DAWN ON A MID-July morning, the stallion's glossy coat gleamed like white satin. His silvery mane and tail seemed woven of the mist that rose from the field beneath his galloping hooves. His nostrils flared, and his large, dark eyes seemed to shine with a mysterious inner glow. He was the horse of Cambria Porters' dreams – powerful, beautiful, absolutely perfect in every way.

"Oh, Moonracer, how I wish you were real!" Cam whispered, gazing at the poster hanging on the wall beside her bed.

Cam's oldest brother and sister had given her the picture a month ago for her fourteenth birthday. The family had all gathered in the big sunny kitchen of the Porters' farmhouse to watch Cam open her presents – clothing and a portable CD player from her parents, CDs from the twins, Natalie and Nathan, and a small wooden box that Cam's nine-year old sister Ruthie had made herself and decorated with seashells.

Scott and Bonnie had insisted that Cam open their present last. "This is from both of us," Scott said, handing her the large flat package. "I bought it and Bonnie framed it. Happy birthday, Cam."

"I'm afraid you won't be able to ride him, but he'll have to do until the real thing comes along," Bonnie added as Cam eagerly began unwrapping their gift.

When she saw the picture, Cam caught her breath. "He's gorgeous!" she exclaimed. "He's the most beautiful horse I ever saw! Thanks, guys." Leaping up from her seat at the table, she gave Scott and Bonnie each a big hug.

"I bet I know what you're going to call him," Cam's mother said with a smile. "Moonracer, right?"

Cam laughed. "How did you guess?"

It was no secret to the Porter family that Cam had been horse-crazy almost from the moment she was born. When Cam and her best friend Lacey Vining were little, instead of having imaginary playmates the way some children did they each had an imaginary horse. Lacey immediately named her prancing ebony steed Black Beauty, but it took Cam a lot longer to figure out what to call her milk-white stallion.

Lacey suggested Thunderhead, like the magnificent white horse in the old movie the girls had seen and loved on TV, but somehow it just didn't feel right. Maybe a secondhand name was good enough for Lacey's make-believe horse, but Cam wanted something extra special. Then one night while she lay in bed looking through her window at the clouds scudding past a silvery full moon the word Moonracer suddenly popped into her head, and she fell asleep knowing that she'd found the perfect name at last. Cam and Lacey had pretended to ride Black Beauty and Moonracer all over the eastern end of Long Island, from the Porters' farm near the village of Shorehaven where Lacey lived to the lighthouse at Montauk Point and back. They'd had so much fun ...

Now as the rising sun filled Cam's little room with rosy light she smiled, remembering those long-ago days. Cam and Lacey had eventually outgrown their make-believe mounts, of course, but not their passion for horses. When they were older, they both took riding lessons at a local stable and dreamed of the day when they would have horses of their own.

Cam sighed. Much as she loved the picture of the white stallion, Moonracer was still just a fantasy. But Lacey didn't have to dream anymore, because back in March for her fourteenth birthday her parents had given her a sturdy little roan mare named Speckles.

Turning her head, Cam focused on a framed photograph on her bureau. Mrs. Vining had taken it shortly after Lacey's birthday. Cam, blond, freckled, and beaming, stood on one side of Speckles, while dark-haired Lacey stood on the other holding the mare's halter. Lacey was grinning from ear to ear and her braces positively sparkled in the early-spring sunlight. Plump, placid Speckles certainly didn't resemble Lacey's imaginary Black Beauty in the least, but she was a real live horse and Lacey was crazy about her.

For the first and only time in all the years they'd known each other, Cam couldn't help envying her best friend. She knew perfectly well that, unlike the Vinings, her parents couldn't afford to buy her a horse. Farming was a seasonal business and chancy at best, and with six kids to feed, clothe, and educate – Bonnie was a junior at Halsey College, Scott hoped to go there the following year, and the sixteen-year-old twins would be next – there was no money to spare for luxuries. Lacey on the other hand was an only child, and Vinings' Hardware was the largest and most successful store of its kind in Shorehaven. Lacey wasn't exactly spoiled, but her parents did tend to buy her anything she wanted.

Just then Jupiter, the largest and fattest of the Porter's three large fat cats, stalked through the half-open door of Cam's room and leaped onto her bed, settling his considerable bulk on her chest.

"Good morning, Jupiter," Cam said to the cat, laying her cheek against his soft fur and stroking his back. "I know you understand. You see, I'm not exactly *jealous* of Lacey. It's just that I hardly see her anymore. But we're still best friends – at least, I hope we are."

The clock radio on her bedside table began playing softly, signaling that it was five thirty and time to get up. Deciding to ignore it for the moment, Cam folded her arms behind her head and stared up at a crack in the ceiling, frowning as she thought about the past few months.

Things hadn't been all that bad to begin with. In fact, Cam was almost as thrilled about Speckles as Lacey was. When they weren't in school they spent every spare minute at Seabreeze Stables, where Lacey's parents boarded the mare. Cam loved helping her friend groom Speckles, and Lacey was more than happy to let Cam ride her horse whenever she wanted.

But in April things began to change. Now that the growing season had begun, Cam's family needed her to help with farm chores. Most days she had to go home right after school, so she wasn't able to spend nearly as much time with Lacey and Speckles as she had before. Soon Lacey began talking about some other girls from school who boarded their horses at the same stable.

"Carla Luchese, Marjorie Ralston, and Diane Steinberg all

belong to this riding club called the South Shore Centaurs," Lacey told Cam one day at lunch in the cafeteria. "We saw the Centaurs in Shorehaven's Santa Claus Parade right after Thanksgiving last year, remember?"

Cam nodded. She remembered very well. The horses had been decked out with sparkling Christmas garlands, and both horses and riders wore bright-red Santa hats on their heads.

"Well, guess what? They've asked me to join!" Lacey said excitedly. "There are seven girls in the club, but the others don't go to Shorehaven Junior High. They live in Brightwater and they board their horses somewhere else, so I haven't met them yet. Anyway, the Centaurs go on trail rides, and picnics on the beach, and sometimes they even ride all the way to Montauk, the way we used to pretend to do when we were little kids. Isn't that terrific?"

"Yeah, terrific." Cam tried to sound enthusiastic, but it wasn't easy. "I guess you're going to join, right?"

Lacey laughed. "You'd better believe it! I've already told them I would. I'm going to my first meeting Saturday evening at Carla's house – we're going to make plans for the Memorial Day parade and figure out what the Centaurs will do over the spring and summer."

"I thought you and I were going to the movies Saturday night," Cam said in a small voice. "Bonnie's going to drive us to the East Hampton Cinema to see *Return of the Black Stallion*."

Lacey's face fell. "Oh, Cam, I completely forgot." She wailed. "I hate to back out on you, but could we see it some other time? This meeting's really important to me." Then she brightened. "Hey, I just had a great idea! Why don't you come to Carla's with me and then sleep over at my house? We could see the movie on Sunday instead."

9

"I don't think so," Cam said. "What's the point of my coming to a Centaurs' meeting? I hardly know Carla, Diane, and Marjorie, and I don't have a horse so I can't become a member. I'd just sit there feeling really out of place. Know what I mean?"

"Yeah, I guess I do," Lacey said with a sigh. "But it would be so much more fun if you could join. We've always done everything together. Tell you what," she added impulsively. "I don't really have to go to that meeting – there'll be plenty more. After all, you're my best friend, and best friends come first. We'll see *Return of the Black Stallion* the way we planned."

Cam shook her head. "No, Lacey, it's okay, honest. I'll see if Scott can drive us to the movies on Sunday afternoon instead."

"Well, if you're sure you don't mind ..."

"I'm sure," Cam said, smiling, " And on the way to East Hampton, you can fill me in on the Centaurs' plans."

So that's what they did. From the moment she got into Scott's beat-up old Chevy until the movie began Lacey chattered away about the riding club, and as Cam listened her spirits sank lower and lower. What with all the activities Lacey glowingly described, it was obvious that the South Shore Centaurs would be taking up most of her weekends until school let out in June. Over the summer, however, the club planned some outings and excursions during the week, and Lacey pointed out that she and Cam could do things together on Saturday and Sunday.

But from Memorial Day to Labor Day Cam and every member of her family, even little Ruthie, worked at the Porters' roadside stand along Montauk Highway, selling their organically grown vegetables, fruits and flowers, eggs from their free-range chickens, and Mrs. Porter's baked goods and preserves to the tourists. As long as it didn't rain weekends were the busiest – and most profitable – times of all, so Cam seldom had a sunny Saturday or Sunday free. She'd even missed Lacey's first appearance as a Centaur in the Memorial Day parade.

"You know something, Jupiter?" Cam said to the cat, who was contentedly dozing right under her chin. "So far this summer I've hardly ridden Speckles at all, and Lacey and I have gone to the beach exactly twice!"

Jupiter opened one yellow eye and yawned so widely that Cam was sure she could see his tonsils. She grinned. "Am I boring you, you lazy old thing? Well, *excuuuuse* me!"

Cam's bedroom door suddenly burst open, and Natalie poked her head in. "Cam, why are you still in bed? It's almost six!" She shouted. "Daddy and Scott are already picking the corn, Ruthie's helping Nate with the tomatoes, and Mom's having a fit because the new oven just pooped out so she has to bake all the cinnamon rolls in the old one. Bonnie's gathering the eggs, and in case you've forgotten, you and I are on breakfast detail, so *get a move on* because I need your help!"

Cam quickly sat up. "Chill out, Nat. I'm moving, I'm moving!" she said, dumping an indignant Jupiter onto the floor. "Sorry, Jup," she said over her shoulder as she headed for the bathroom. "Duty calls!"

Less than an hour later the family had finished their breakfast. Cam's father, Scott, Ruthie, Bonnie, and Nathan had returned to their chores, and Cam was loading the dishwasher while Natalie helped their mother take freshly baked rolls from the oven and place them on racks to cool.

"I just can't understand it," Ruth-Ann Porter muttered, scowling at the brand-new oven. "The thing worked perfectly fine until today. Thank goodness I baked my bread last night! Wouldn't you know it would decide to break down right in the middle of the tourist season when I've promised to deliver dozens of rolls to the Maidstone Inn? If we can't get them there in time, they'll never give me another order!"

"Relax, Mom," Natalie soothed. "It's still early. Cam can take Scott's place in the cornfield, and Scott will deliver the rolls long before anybody at the Maidstone is ready for breakfast. Those vacationers probably won't wake up for hours yet."

"I guess you're right," their mother said with a sigh. "At least the oven's still under warranty so we won't have to pay for repairs."

Cam closed the dishwasher and turned it on. "What's the schedule today, Mom?" she asked.

Mrs. Porter peered nearsightedly at the chart posted on the refrigerator door. "I wonder what I did with my glasses. Let's see – it's Saturday the fourteenth, right?" Cam nodded. "Okay. You, Nat, and Ruthie will be taking the first shift at the stand. Bonnie's going to help me make jam, and that'll probably take us until early afternoon, so she won't be able to start selling until two or three. But Nate and Scott will relieve you girls at around one and then you'll be free for the rest of the day."

"Hey, great!" Natalie said. Turning to Cam, she suggested, "If I can talk Scott into letting me borrow his precious wheels, why don't you, me, and Ruthie go to the beach this afternoon?"

"Good idea," Cam said. "Maybe Lacey could come, too – if she's not horsing around with her new pals, that is. I'll phone her when we come home for lunch."

12

"If you do go, you'll have to bring the car back by five so Scott can get to his job at the gas station," their mother reminded them as she slid several more trays of cinnamon rolls into the oven. "And speaking of Scott, you'd better make tracks for the cornfield, Cam. This is the last batch, and as soon as it's done, your brother can take them to the inn."

Cam dashed out the kitchen door, almost running into Bonnie, who was on her way in with two baskets full of brown eggs.

"Watch it!" Bonnie warned. "Nobody's going to buy pre-scrambled eggs!"

Cam just laughed and broke into a jog trot across the big backyard. Sailor, the Porters' black Labrador, frisked along beside her as she loped past the tomato patch. Cam waved to Ruthie and Nate, who were busy harvesting the many different varieties, from tiny red and yellow cherries to huge scarlet beefsteaks. Near the chicken coops Sailor shot off in pursuit of an imaginary rabbit and disappeared around the corner of the barn, leaving Cam to run on by herself.

When Cam reached the cornfield she stopped for a moment, looking for her father's pickup truck since Scott and Hal Porter were hidden among the tall green stalks. After she had delivered her message and Scott headed back to the house, Cam helped her father pick ears of the sweet yellow and white corn called Butter-and-Sugar and tossed them into big wooden crates. As each crate was filled Mr. Porter hefted it into the back of the pickup. Even though it was still early, the sun was so hot that Cam was soon dripping with sweat.

"It's going to be a scorcher today, that's for sure," her father said, pausing to take off his broad-brimmed straw hat and mop his freckled forehead with a bandanna.

13

"Tomorrow's supposed to be the same, so the stand ought to do pretty well. Good thing, too, considering how rainy the past few weeks have been."

"Maybe we ought to raise our prices, Dad," Cam suggested. "Nate says the Zalefskis charge a dollar for three ears of corn, but we sell our customers four ears for the same price."

Mr. Porter shook his head. "I don't want to gouge the tourists no matter how much money they have. The Porters have never been buccaneers."

He grinned at Cam. And she grinned back, delivering the punch line of one of his favorite jokes. "Yeah – *a buck an ear* is a heck of a lot to pay for corn!"

Laughing, her father put his straw hat back on his head at a jaunty angle. "You're a chip off the old block, honey," he said. "Come on – we only have one more crate to fill, and then we'll pick up the rest of the stuff and take off for the highway. On a beautiful day like this, there are bound to be thousands of folks getting an early start on their vacation, and we don't want to keep them waiting."

Mr. Porter loaded the last crate into the truck, then got into the driver's seat. Cam climbed in next to him.

"I'm sure glad we don't live up-island in some dirty old city and have to spend hours stuck in a car just to get some fresh air and sunshine," she said. "I guess it wasn't so bad in the old days, though, when everybody used horses to get where they were going."

Looking out over the flat green fields that stretched as far as the eye could see she mused aloud. "Sometimes I wish I lived back then, before smelly cars polluted the atmosphere and rich people started buying up all the land out here and building fancy houses all over the place."

Cam wrinkled her nose at the sight of several new houses on the distant horizon. "I bet by the time I'm grown up, there won't be any farms left – except ours." Turning to her father, she asked anxiously, "You'll never sell our land, will you, Daddy? Not even to send the rest of us to college?"

"No, Cam, I never will," Mr. Porter assured her. "That's a promise. This farm has been in the Porter family for five generations, and your mother and I are not about to let some developer gobble it up. There's not enough money in the world to make us change our minds. We'll manage somehow. We always have." As the pickup jounced down the rutted dirt track through the cornfield and turned onto Skunk Hollow Road, he added, "I just wish there weren't so many things you kids have to do without."

"Like what?" Cam asked. "If you ask me, we're pretty lucky. So what if we're not rich? We've got everything we need."

Her father patted her knee with a callused, sunburned hand. "No argument there. But I was thinking about decent cars for Bonnie and Scott, among other things. Those rattletraps they drive are held together with spit and hope. And then there's the horse you've always wanted. I know how much you'd like to join that riding club Lacey belongs to, honey, and I hope *you* know that I'd buy you a horse if I could."

"Sure I do. Don't worry about it, Daddy," Cam said quickly. "I'd love to have my own horse, but I don't really *need* one. And who knows – maybe someday after I graduate from college and get a job, I'll have a whole stable full of horses."

"If that's your plan, it'll have to be a pretty darn good job," Mr. Porter said with a wry grin.

Cam laughed. "I guess you're right. Anyway, I was just kidding. I wouldn't want dozens of horses, just one – a beautiful pure-white stallion exactly like Moonracer ..."

Her voice trailed off and she gazed into space, picturing herself on Moonracer's bare back galloping in the surf along the ocean beach at sunset. His gait was so smooth that it was like floating on a cloud, and his silken mane and tail streamed behind him like banners.

The pickup jolted to a stop next to the tomato patch, and her father's voice broke into Cam's thoughts. "Daydreaming again, honey?"

"Yeah, I guess I was," Cam admitted, smiling sheepishly. "Sorry."

"It's perfectly okay to daydream as long as you don't confuse your dreams with reality," Mr. Porter said gently. "But whatever those dreams are, I hope they all come true."

Cam leaned over and kissed his weathered cheek. "Thanks, Daddy, I love you!"

"Love you too."

"Hey, you guys, are you gonna sit there all day?" Nathan called, staggering over to the truck under the weight of a huge box of Big Boy tomatoes. "I could use a little help here – make that a *lot* of help."

As Cam and her father got out of the pickup, Ruthie raced toward the house hollering, "Mom, Daddy and Cam are back!"

"Where's Nat?" Mr. Porter asked Nathan, taking the carton of Big Boys from him.

"In the barn with about a ton of zucchini. She says you can pick her up there."

"Okay. Cam, how about giving your mother and Bonnie a hand with the flowers, bread, and eggs? After Nate and I finish loading the vegetables, I'll take Nat to the stand and then come back for you and Ruthie. Think you can be ready to go in about half an hour?"

"No problem," Cam said.

She trotted across the yard, the image of the white stallion still vivid in her mind. *Someday I'll have a horse like that*, Cam vowed to herself. *I only hope when that day comes I won't be too old and decrepit to ride him!*

TWO

BY NINE O'CLOCK A STEADY STREAM OF CARS
filled with eager beachgoers was flowing eastward along
the narrow, two-lane Montauk Highway. Attracted by the
big green and white sign that read 'PORTERS' PRODUCE
– LONG ISLAND'S FINEST – HOME-GROWN, ALL
ORGANIC, PESTICIDE-FREE', many drivers pulled off
onto the shoulder to stock up for the weekend.

Cam, Natalie, and Ruthie, wearing oversized white
T-shirts that Bonnie had lettered in green with the same
message as the sign, had seldom been busier. Natalie
handled the cash box behind the counter of the farm stand
and also sold Mrs. Porter's baked goods and preserves.
Cam and Ruthie worked in front, helping customers with
their purchases.

"How much is the corn, miss?" a deeply tanned woman
wearing a colorful print sundress asked Cam.

"Four for a dollar, two-fifty a dozen."

The woman's equally tanned husband nodded
approvingly. "Good price. Much cheaper than Zalefskis'.
Let's get two dozen, honey," he told his wife. "On second
thought, better make it three dozen. We'll need that many
for our clambake tonight."

"Just pick out the ones you want and put them in here," Cam said, handing them each a basket. "You can pay my sister at the counter, and she'll bag them for you."

As she turned away to help some other customers, Ruthie hurried over to her. "Cam, that lady over there wants to know if she can buy a T-shirt," she whispered. "Can I sell her mine?"

Laughing, Cam said, "No, silly! You don't have anything on underneath it. Do you want to be arrested for indecent exposure?"

Ruthie giggled. "I guess not. But if Bonnie made some more shirts like ours, I bet lots of people would buy them."

"You know, that's not the worst idea in the world." Cam replied. "It would be great advertising for the stand, too. Let's talk to Bonnie about it when we get home, okay?"

"Okay, I'll try to sell the lady something else."

Ruthie trotted off. Noticing that one of their regular customers, a frail, elderly man who walked with a cane, was having trouble lifting his overflowing basket, Cam hurried to his side.

"Morning, Mr. Brennan," she said cheerfully. "Can I carry that for you?"

"Thank you, Cambria. That's one of the things I like about this place," he said as they walked to the stand. "The Porters always render service with a smile. Believe me, my dear, you don't get much of that sort of thing these days. Your mother and father are both well, I trust?"

"Yes, they're fine. Mom's at home today making jam – raspberry-peach, I think."

"Then I shall have to come back tomorrow and buy some," Mr. Brennan stated. "I dearly love your mother's jam. Which reminds me, I must buy some of her wonderful bread or I won't have anything to spread it on."

Cam placed his basket on the counter. "Nat, Mr. Brennan wants a loaf of Mom's bread. Whole-grain, right?" she asked the old man.

"Yes, dear child, whole-grain," he said. "Good morning, Natalie. Pray tell, how much do I owe you for this bounty from your fields and hearth?"

As he took out his wallet, Cam's eyes met her sister's and they both grinned. They loved the old fashioned way Mr. Brennan talked.

Just then a hatchet-faced woman wearing too-tight shorts, enormous sunglasses, and a lot of jangling jewelry tapped Cam on the shoulder. "Miss! Miss! How about paying some attention to your other customers?" she said irritably. "I don't have all day, y'know!"

Too bad everybody's not as nice as Mr. Brennan, Cam thought. Pasting a polite smile on her face, she said, "Right away, ma'am. What can I do for you?"

Teetering on high-heeled sandals, the woman led the way to an ancient wooden buckboard where the cut flowers were displayed. Ruthie was standing beside the wagon, her arms folded across her chest and a stubborn expression on her freckled face.

"Well, to begin with, you can tell this kid here to give me a break on the price of those crummy zinnias," the woman snapped. "She says they're five dollars a bunch, but anybody can see they're wilted! I'm not going to pay that much for a bunch of wilted zinnias, nosiree. Now if you'll give me two bunches for five bucks, you've got a deal."

"They are not wilted!" Ruthie muttered. "They're fresh as anything. We just picked them yesterday evening!"

20

Cam shot her a warning glance, then turned to the woman she had privately nicknamed Mrs. Loudmouth. "I'm sorry, ma'am," she said sweetly, "but I'm afraid I can't do that. Five dollars is a fair price for two dozen zinnias – you won't do better anywhere along the highway." She couldn't resist adding, "Besides, if you don't think the flowers are fresh and you don't like the way they look, why would you want to buy twice as many of them?"

"Well, I never!" Mrs. Loudmouth sputtered. "I'll tell you what's fresh! *You're* fresh, young lady, and so's that kid!"

She stood there for a moment glaring at Cam and Ruthie. Then she snatched the nearest bunch of zinnias, shoved them into her basket, and teetered off to pay for them.

Ruthie clapped her hand over her mouth to stifle her giggles. As soon as Mrs. Loudmouth was out of earshot, she said, "Boy, what a cheapskate! She knew there was nothing wrong with those flowers. She just didn't want to pay full price."

Cam shrugged. "I guess it takes all kinds. But I'm sure glad we don't run into *her* kind very often."

"Me too!" Ruthie said.

Suddenly, with a loud screeching of brakes the cars that had been whizzing past the farm stand came to an abrupt half. All the people who had been busily filling their baskets with Porters' Produce hurried to the side of the road, craning their necks as they peered down the highway trying to see what the problem was. Cam and Ruthie followed the crowd.

"Gee, Cam, what do you suppose happened?" Ruthie asked. "There must have been an accident!"

"I don't think so," Cam said. "I didn't hear a crash or anything."

21

Ruthie's eyes widened. "Maybe a car hit a person! You know how Mom and Daddy are always telling us never, *never* to cross the highway on a day like this when there's so much traffic. What if somebody did and they got *killed* and they're lying there all bloody and squashed with their head busted open and –"

"Stop it, Ruthie!" Cam gave her a shake. "I bet some car's engine just overheated and it stalled out. Things like that happen all the time in hot weather."

"Will somebody please tell me what's going on?" Natalie yelled from her post behind the counter.

"Nobody knows," Cam yelled back. "I'll go take a look."

"I'm coming with you," Ruthie announced. "I've never seen a bloody dead person before except on TV!"

Cam stared at her sister in astonishment. "You're a little ghoul, Ruthie, you know that? You are not coming with me. Stay right here, and don't you dare move a single inch, understand? I'll be right back. And while I'm gone, no matter how much anybody offers for your T-shirt, *don't sell it*!"

Ruthie stuck out her lower lip. "Oh, okay. I promise. But if there is a bloody dead person, you have to tell me all about it!"

Cam began jogging along the sandy shoulder of the highway, skirting the cluster of rubberneckers who seemed to share Ruthie's fascination with blood and gore. As she ran she put her hands over her ears, but she couldn't shut out the blare of horns blown by impatient drivers caught in the monumental traffic jam.

"Let's get this show on the road!" bellowed a red-faced man, sticking his head out of the window of his car.

A woman wearing a floppy straw hat leaned out of her convertible and called to Cam, "Any idea what's happening up ahead?"

22

Cam just shook her head and kept on jogging.

And then she saw it.

Cam stopped in her tracks. She blinked, hardly able to believe her eyes. Standing stock-still in the middle of the Montauk Highway was a horse. But what a horse! Cam had never seen anything like it before. The creature looked more like a skinny, shaggy, long-legged brown bear. Its four cracked, overgrown hooves were firmly planted on the hot black macadam and its ears were laid back. It glared defiantly at the noisy gas-guzzlers, as if daring them to challenge its right to be there.

The horse suddenly caught sight of Cam. As it swung its large head in her direction, she noticed that its left eye was bluish-white.

"That is the ugliest horse I have ever seen in my entire life!" she muttered under her breath.

The driver of the car directly in front of the animal yelled something at Cam that she couldn't hear.

"Excuse me?" she said coming over to him and bending down. The man was young, tanned, and muscular with longish blond hair, and there were a couple of surfboards strapped to the roof of his car.

"I said does that thing belong to you?" he shouted in her ear.

Cam shook her head vigorously. "I never saw it before this very minute."

"Well, do you think you could get it off the road?"

Cam glanced doubtfully at the horse. It looked as if it had taken root where it stood. "I guess I could give it a try," she said, "but I'm not sure I can do it by myself. I don't suppose you'd like to give me a hand?"

"Who, me?" The guy looked shocked. "No way! I ride waves, not horses. That is a horse, isn't it?"

"More or less," Cam said with a grimace. "Well, let me see what I can do."

Cam straightened up and squared her shoulders. She was about to approach the animal when she saw a balding, heavyset farmer in faded overalls striding across the highway from the opposite side. Although Cam had never actually met him, she knew who he was. His name was Sam Barnett, and according to Cam's father he was famous for his short temper. At the moment he looked furious.

"You no-good, walleyed, flea-bitten bag of bones!" Mr. Barnett roared at the horse, waving the stout stick he carried. "This is the last time you're gonna get into trouble! Soon as I get you home, I swear I'm gonna sell you for dog food! I should've done it long ago."

Cam gasped. No matter how weird looking the animal was, it was still a horse, and she was horrified at the thought of its being killed and canned. She always scanned the label of every can of dog food her mother bought for Sailor to make sure it didn't contain horsemeat.

"You wouldn't really do that, Mr. Barnett, would you?" she cried, running over to him.

He glared at her. "What do you care? If he was dog food, he'd be useful for a change. As it is, Spunky's good for nothing except tying up traffic from here to Montauk Point!"

"His name's Spunky?" Cam asked.

"Yep. Anyways, it used to be. Most of the time I call him Plug-Ugly, 'cause that's what he is." Mr. Barnett looked at her more closely. "Say, you're one of Hal Porter's kids, aint'cha?"

"Yes, sir. I'm Cambria, Cam for short."

The honking was even louder now. Several people who

24

had gotten out of their cars started chanting in unison, "CLEAR – THE – ROAD! CLEAR – THE – ROAD!"

"Tell you what, Cam," the farmer said. "You scared of horses?"

"Oh, no, not at all," Cam replied quickly.

"Good. You take the front end and I'll take the rear. Maybe between the two of us we can get ol' Plug over to the shoulder."

That sounded like a good idea to Cam. Grabbing hold of Plug-Ugly's worn leather halter, she tugged with all her might while Mr. Barnett swatted his rump with the stick and yelled, "Get moving!"

Cam cringed at the sound of the blows, but the horse didn't even seem to feel them. The only thing about him that moved was his scruffy tail as he switched away an annoying fly. They tried time after time with the same result: Plug-Ugly refused to budge an inch.

"Stubbornest animal on the face of the earth, and that's the truth," the farmer grumbled, wiping his sweating face on his sleeve. Turning to Cam, he raised his voice. "Let's do it again, and this time put your back into it!"

"I *was* putting my back into it," Cam said irritably. "You don't have to yell at me – I'm doing the best I can!"

She wasn't usually rude to grown-ups, but the heat was getting to her, and so was Mr. Barnett's attitude. After all, she was doing *him* a favor, not the other way around. It wasn't *her* stupid, ugly horse that was standing like a statue in the middle of the highway!

"Sorry, sis," he said sheepishly. "Don't mind me. My bark's a lot worse'n my bite – most of the time anyways."

Ashamed of her outburst, Cam said, "I'm sorry too, Mr. Barnett. I shouldn't have snapped at you like that, but

25

it seems like we're getting nowhere fast. Maybe we ought to try a different approach."

"Maybe so, but I'm fresh out of dynamite." The farmer sighed.

Cam couldn't help grinning. "I was thinking of something a little less drastic. What if we tried persuasion instead of force?"

"Persuasion? With that ornery animal?" Mr. Barnett snorted.

"Well, it wouldn't hurt to try." Cam pointed out. She hurried back to the surfer and shouted over the honking and chanting. "Excuse me, but you wouldn't happen to have an apple or a carrot with you, by any chance?"

The guy stopped leaning on his horn and scowled at her. "Why? Getting hungry? No wonder – you've been fooling around with that horse so long that it must be almost noon!"

"It's not for me," Cam said patiently. "It's for the horse. I want to see if I can lure him off the road with it."

"Hey, in that case, be my guest." He took an apple from the cooler on the seat next to him and tossed it to her. "This better work, kid, because if it doesn't, I just might run the darn thing down. I mean, I brake for animals, like my bumper sticker says, but this is ridiculous!"

"Thanks!" Cam sang out. "I hope you catch some really terrific waves!"

Returning to Plug-Ugly, she placed the apple on the flat of her palm and held it under his nose. The horse sniffed at it suspiciously.

"Smells nice, doesn't it, boy?" Cam said in a soft, wheedling voice. "Wouldn't you like to take a great big bite out of it? Well, you can have the whole thing. All you have to do is follow me."

Still holding out the apple, she began to back slowly toward the shoulder. Plug-Ugly's flattened ears slowly came forward. He followed the apple with his eyes and stretched his neck, but his hooves stayed where they were.

"This ain't gonna work," Mr. Barnett muttered.

Cam ignored him. "Come on, Plug," she urged. "It's all yours if you'll just follow me."

The horse flicked his ears and switched his tail. He shifted his weight from side to side. Then he took one stumbling step. He took another step, and then another. Cam kept walking backward, murmuring. "That's right. Keep moving, fella. Just a little farther ..."

Suddenly Plug-Ugly stopped dead. He laid back his ears again and snatched at the apple with his teeth, but Cam kept it out of his reach.

"Oh, no," she said firmly. "No reward until you're completely off the road."

Giving her a baleful look, the horse tossed his head and snorted. Cam thought he sounded exactly like Sam Barnett. At last, Plug-Ugly started walking, more briskly this time, and as soon as he reached the shoulder of the road she let him take the apple from her hand.

The chanters burst into cheers, the horns stopped honking, and car engines began revving up. Mr. Barnett hardly had time to join his horse and Cam on the south side of the highway before the traffic began moving again.

Scratching his bald head, the farmer said, "I gotta hand it to you, kid, I never would've thought Plug would go for the old apple trick."

"He knows a good thing when he sees it, that's all," Cam replied. "He sure is ugly, but he's not dumb."

"You may be right about that," Mr. Barnett agreed

grimly. "Fact is, when it comes to making mischief, I guess you'd have to call Plug some kind of a genius."

He took hold of the horse's halter and gave it a yank. When Plug responded by nipping at his arm, Mr. Barnett smacked him on the nose. After a brief struggle, Plug reluctantly began plodding after him in the direction of the farm stand. Cam walked along beside Mr. Barnett, being careful to keep her distance from the horse's strong yellow teeth.

"He wasn't always ugly, though," the farmer went on. "When I bought him for Mandy – that's my daughter – she wasn't much older than you are, and Plug was a pretty decent-looking four-year-old gelding. Mandy was crazy about him. She's the one who named him Spunky, and she used to ride him all the time. When Mandy got married and moved out of state, she wouldn't let me get rid of him, so I turned him out to pasture to fend for himself."

"How long ago was that?" Cam asked.

Mr. Barnett had to think about that for a minute. "Well, let's see … Mandy's twenty-four, so it must be going on two years now, and he's been nothing but trouble ever since."

"This horse has been on his own for two whole years?" Cam exclaimed. "No wonder he's such a mess!"

"Now hang on there, young lady!" he blustered. "Like I told you, keeping Plug wasn't my idea. It was Mandy's. The last thing I need is some escape-artist horse that keeps breaking out of his pasture and running all over the South Fork. I got a lot more important things to do than chase after the darned animal!"

"Maybe if you told your daughter what a problem Plug is, she wouldn't mind if you sold him," Cam suggested.

"Sold him? Ha! That's funny!" But Mr. Barnett wasn't laughing. "Look at him! Who'd buy a horse that looks like that?" Considering the appearance of the large, shaggy beast, Cam admitted he had a point. "Anyways, it ain't just the way Plug looks. You've seen how he acts. He's mean as sin and stubborn as a mule."

"Well, now that you've got him back, I guess you'll have to figure out what to do about him," Cam said.

Mr. Barnett jerked on Plug's halter again, muttering something that Cam thought sounded very much like "dog food."

"No!" she cried. "you mustn't do that!"

"I guess I won't. Mandy'd pitch a fit if I did." He sighed. "But I tell you, sis, I gotta get rid of this animal somehow. Heck, for two cents I'd *give* him away!"

It took a couple of seconds for Mr. Barnett's words to sink in. When they finally did, Cam said, "You mean it? You'd really do that?"

He nodded. "Yep, I sure would if I could find some sucker who'd take him."

Cam turned and looked at the horse as he shambled along behind Mr. Barnett. *There's no doubt about it*, she thought. *Plug-Ugly's the perfect name for him. He's about as far from Moonracer as an animal can get and still be a horse. He might as well be a creature from another planet!*

She narrowed her eyes. *Still, if he was cleaned up and groomed, and his hooves were trimmed, maybe …*

Cam shook her head impatiently. *Forget it!* She told herself. *I must be crazy! Like Grandma always says, you can't make a silk purse out of a sow's ear.*

But Cam had a very vivid imagination, and a picture suddenly formed in her mind, complete with sound effects.

29

The South Shore Centaurs were trotting along a country lane. Cam could hear the girls' happy voices and the soft clop-clop of their horses' hooves. And right in the midst of them, riding next to Lacey and Speckles, was Cam on a shiny brown gelding with one walleye.

Okay, so he's not beautiful like Moonracer and he has a nasty disposition, she thought. *At least he's a horse. And if I had my own horse, I could join the Centaurs!*

"Mr. Barnett," she said, "you just found yourself a sucker!"

THREE

SAM BARNETT GAVE ONE OF HIS HORSEY SNORTS.
"OH, yeah? Where? Who?"

"Here. Me," Cam said.

"You?" The farmer threw back his head and laughed.
"That's a good one, that is!"

Cam frowned. "What's so funny? Were you just joking
when you said you'd give Plug away?"

"Well, I guess I meant it, but I never thought anybody'd
take me up on it, least of all a kid like you." Mr. Barnett
admitted. "What the heck would you want him for?"

"To ride, of course," she replied eagerly. "I've always
wanted a horse of my own, and even though Plug's nothing
like what I had in mind, he is a horse. So if you meant what
you said about getting rid of him, I'll take him. What do
you say, Mr. Barnett?"

He gaped at her. "You're really serious, aint'cha?"

Cam nodded, "I sure am." Thinking fast, she added,
"But I don't want you to give him to me because you might
change your mind and decide to take him back. I'll *buy* him
from you – for two cents!"

"Terrific!" Cam stuck out her hand and Mr. Barnett shook it.

They had reached the farm stand by now, and several

startled customers turned to gawk as Cam led the farmer and his reluctant horse over to the buckboard filled with flowers. "Could you wait here, please?" she said to Mr. Barnett. "I'll get the money right now."

As Cam headed for the counter, Ruthie raced up to her. "What took you so long? What happened? Was there an accident? Was anybody killed?" she cried. Glancing over at Mr. Barnett, she added in a whisper, "Who's that man?" She pointed to Plug. "And where did *that* come from?"

"Tell you later," Cam said, grinning, "I have to talk to Nat."

With Ruthie at her heels, she hurried over to their older sister. "Nat, I need two pennies," she said, "and a piece of paper and a pencil!"

"What for?"

"Never mind. Please just give them to me, okay?"

With a shrug, Natalie did as she asked. Cam grabbed the pennies and scribbled a few lines on the paper while Ruthie watched, a puzzled frown on her face. Ruthie trotted after her as she ran back to Mr. Barnett.

"This is a bill of sale," Cam explained. "You have to sign it so everything will be legal."

Chuckling to himself, Mr. Barnett wrote his name on the paper. Then he gave it back to Cam and pocketed the pennies she thrust at him. "Here he is, signed, sealed, and delivered," he said, handing her the gelding's halter. "Good luck with him, kid – you're sure gonna need it!"

Still chuckling, Mr. Barnett took advantage of a gap in the traffic and lumbered across the highway.

Plug didn't seem to notice or care. He was much more interested in eyeing the nearest bunch of zinnias. Cam yanked on his halter just in time to prevent his taking a mouthful of flowers.

"What's going on, Cam?" Ruthie whined. "Why did that man leave his ugly horse with you?"

"Because it isn't Mr. Barnett's horse anymore," Cam said. "It's mine! I just bought it from him."

"You're kidding!"

"Nope. Look," Cam held out the piece of paper.

Ruthie snatched it and as she read the words aloud, her eyes almost popped out of her head. "I, Mister Sam Barnett, do hereby sell my horse Spunky, also known as Plug-Ugly, to Miss Cambria Porter for the sum of two cents cash." As Cam took the paper and tucked it into her shorts pocket for safekeeping, Ruthie gasped, "Oh, wow! I'm gonna go tell Nat!"

She spun around, about to sprint off toward the counter, but Cam grabbed her T-shirt, holding her back. "I'll tell her myself in a minute. But first, see if you can find me a long piece of rope – a *strong* piece. I have to get back to work, and I want to tie Plug to that tree over there so he'll be out of the way until I can take him home."

"Home? Oh, wow!" Ruthie said again. "Wait till Mom and Daddy find out about this! They'll *murder you*!"

Sounding more confident than she felt, Cam said, "No, they won't. Now will you please go look for that rope?"

Until that very moment, her parents' reaction hadn't entered Cam's mind, but now it occurred to her that Ruthie might have a point. It wasn't that they didn't want her to have a horse – her father had said only a few hours ago that he wished he could buy one for her – but they might be less than thrilled when Cam showed up with Plug-Ugly.

Well, no sense worrying about that now. she said to herself. *I'll just have to take it one step at a time.*

33

While Cam hung on to Plug, waiting for Ruthie to come back with the rope, she couldn't help being aware of the curious glances she and the horse were getting. Glances weren't all they got. Cam heard some snickers, too. Several people made jokes about Plug's scruffy appearance, but at least one of them seemed outraged.

A stout woman wearing a flowered muumuu and clutching a bunch of carrots marched up to her. "Is that your horse, young lady?" she asked. When Cam nodded, the woman angrily waved the carrots at her. Plug was very interested in the carrots. "You ought to be ashamed of yourself, letting the poor beast get into such pitiful condition. Neglect and abuse, that's what it is!"

"Well, you see, ma'am, I just –" Cam began, but the carrot woman cut her off.

"No excuses!" she snapped. "Young people today have no sense of responsibility. If I weren't on vacation, I'd report you to the Humane Society!" Tossing her carrots into the basket she carried, the woman marched off just as Ruthie returned with a length of rope.

"Sorry it took me so long," she said. "I had to tell some people what arugula is."

"That's okay. I had plenty of company while you were gone." Cam sighed. "Thanks, Ruthie."

Fastening the rope to Plug's halter, she dragged him behind the shed and tied him securely to the trunk of a big old tree. Then she stood there for a moment, studying her horse from sloping nose to tangled tail.

"You sure aren't much to look at," Cam told him at last. "And to be perfectly honest, I don't even like you at all!"

Plug snorted, flattened his ears, and deliberately turned around so that she found herself talking to his rear end.

"I guess you don't like me, either," Cam went on. "But you belong to me now, so we'll have to learn to get along somehow. After I get you all cleaned up, you and I are going to join the South Shore Centaurs. And who knows – someday, we might even be friends."

"Cam, what's this Ruthie just told me about you buying a horse from some farmer?" Natalie asked, coming up beside her. She stared incredulously at Plug's furry hindquarters and his matted, burr-infested tail. "Don't tell me that's it!"

Instead of answering her sister's question, Cam said, "Who's minding the store?"

"Scott. He came early with some more lettuce and herbs, so I asked him to cover for me. Cam, will you quit hedging?"

Just then Plug turned around again and gave both girls a dirty look. "*Please* tell me that's not the horse you bought!" Natalie wailed. "It's the ugliest, filthiest animal I ever saw, and what's more, it's blind in one eye!"

"No, he's not. He's just walleyed. His right eye doesn't have enough pigment to make it brown like the other one," Cam explained. With a feeble grin, she added, "And after all, he only cost two cents!"

"Do you mean that's what you wanted those pennies for? Well, if you ask me, you overpaid," Natalie said dryly. "Its owner probably would have paid you to take it off his hands!" She shook her head. "Cambria Elaine Porter, I can't believe you'd pull a stunt like this! And to top it off, you didn't even ask Mom and Dad's permission!"

"Oh, Nat, try to understand," Cam pleaded. "I know it was a crazy thing to do, but I've dreamed of having a horse for so long! And Mr. Barnett threatened to turn Plug into dog food. What was I supposed to do?"

35

"Looks like you traded your dream horse for a nightmare!" Natalie said. "What did you call him just now?"

"Plug, short for Plug-Ugly." Before her sister could make the obvious crack, Cam said, "His name used to be Spunky, but Mr. Barnett, the man I bought him from, changed it. I'm going to change it again though. I mean, Spunky doesn't really suit him, and once he's all groomed and everything he won't be ugly anymore."

Natalie raised her eyebrows. "Wanna bet?" Then she sighed. "Look, Cam, I do understand how you feel – kind of – but I really think you ought to talk to Mom and Dad right away. Ruthie, Scott, and I can take care of the stand, and Nate will be here pretty soon. Why don't you take Plug home now?"

"Well ..." Cam hesitated. "Okay. Guess I might as well get it over with."

As she began untying Plug from the tree, Natalie said more gently, "They may make you give him back, you know. If they do, you've still got Moonracer."

"Yeah, but I can't ride a picture with the Centaurs," Cam said. "I'll have a beautiful horse like Moonracer someday, one I can really love. Until then, Plug's better than nothing." She turned to the gelding and gave a tug on the rope. "Come on, horse. Time to meet the rest of the family."

It took a long time for Cam and Plug-Ugly to reach the Porters' farm. The horse kept stopping every few yards to nibble the greenery by the dirt road, and no matter how hard Cam pulled on the rope, he refused to budge until he was good and ready. While they plodded along in fits and starts, Cam tried to figure out what she would say to her parents when she sprang her big surprise.

36

Look what followed me home? That had worked a few years ago when Scott appeared with Sailor at his heels, but a full-grown horse was a lot different than a half-grown puppy. Besides, it wasn't really true.

Okay, how about the cheerful, positive approach? *Guess what, Daddy and Mom! You know that horse I always wanted? Well, I just bought one, and here he is!*

Cam decided to give up on introductions for the time being and concentrate instead on making up a list of good, solid reasons why her mother and father should allow her to keep Plug. Since money had always been the main obstacle to her owning a horse, she focused on the financial angle.

Number one: Plug was practically free.

Number two: Since we only use the barn for storage, all those stalls are standing empty, so we won't have to pay a fortune to board him the way Lacey does.

Number three: We grow our own hay and corn, so all we'd have to buy is grain and horse chow.

Number four: I've got almost a hundred dollars in my savings account, and I'll turn over all my allowance to pay for having his hooves trimmed and shod, his tack, and anything else he might need.

By the time Cam finally led Plug up the lane to the house, she had convinced herself that the horse's upkeep would cost practically nothing. *Now all I have to do is convince Mom and Daddy*, she thought.

Cam was relieved to see that the pickup was gone. That meant Nathan had already driven off to the farm stand, so she would only have to deal with their parents. After going over her mental list one more time, she turned to Plug.

"I'm going to put you in the barn until I break the

news to my folks," she told him. "After I've explained everything, I'll bring them out to see you. If they're prepared for the way you look, maybe they won't be so shocked. Let's see – Mom and Bonnie are probably in the kitchen. I wonder where Daddy is."

Cam didn't have to wonder long. As she and Plug approached the barn Mr. Porter came out to meet them. Oddly enough, although he looked very serious, he didn't look at all surprised to see his daughter leading a disreputable-looking horse. In fact, it was almost as if he'd been expecting them.

"So that's Sam Barnett's horse, the one he calls Plug-Ugly," he said.

Cam was so dismayed by this unexpected change in her carefully arranged plans that for a moment she couldn't say a single word. She just stared at him, open-mouthed. When she finally found her voice, she said, "How did you know?"

"Sam just left a few minutes ago. He drove over here to drop off a saddle and bridle, and a bucketful of grooming equipment." With a grimace at Plug, Mr. Porter added, "Looks like nobody's used them lately." He turned back to Cam. "Of course, I asked Sam why he was giving me all this stuff when we didn't have a horse, and he told me that as of about an hour ago, we did – or rather, you did. He said you bought this animal from him for two cents. Is that right?"

"Yes, I did," Cam confessed. "I'm sorry, Daddy. I know I should have asked you and Mom first, but you were all the way up here, and I was all the way down there, and everything was such a mess what with the humongous traffic jam and all, and … Well, to tell the truth, I didn't even think about it until after I'd paid Mr. Barnett, and then

38

it was too late." She took a deep breath. "I guess you're pretty mad at me, huh?"

"Well, I'm not particularly pleased," her father said, "but I guess I can't really blame you for jumping at the chance to have your own horse."

"Then I can keep him?" Cam asked eagerly. "Nat said you might make me give him back. You won't will you. Daddy? I know you're worried about the expense, but I've worked it all out in my head, and –"

Mr. Porter held up a hand. "Whoa! We have to discuss this with your mother. Until we decide what to do with him, the horse can stay here in the barn."

Cam followed him inside, hauling Plug after her. It took quite a struggle to get him into one of the stalls, and as soon as she closed and latched the door, the gelding started pawing the ground and kicking at the walls.

"Not very sweet-tempered, is he?" Her father said.

"That's for sure! But he's been out to pasture for two years," Cam replied. "He probably thinks he's in prison or something. He'll calm down in a little while."

"You mean it's been two years since this horse was ridden?" Mr. Porter frowned. "I don't like the sound of that, Cam. He'll most likely be difficult to handle, and you could get hurt."

"No, I won't. Daddy. I'll be very careful," she said. "He's not a bucking bronco, you know. In fact, from what I've seen of him so far, it'll be a miracle if I can even get him to move! Just let me get him a bucket of water and then we'll go talk to Mom, okay?"

"A horse? You bought a horse from Sam Barnett?" Mrs. Porter exclaimed when Cam made her announcement a few minutes later. She collapsed into a wicker armchair on the screened porch where Cam, her parents, and Bonnie had gone to escape the hot, steamy kitchen. "Good heavens! I didn't even know Sam had a horse! When did this happen? Where ...? How ...?"

Bonnie perched on the arm of their mother's chair and patted her shoulder soothingly. "Take it easy, Mom," she said. "If you'll let Cam get a word in edgewise, I'm sure she'll give us all the details."

Cam quickly told the whole story. After she recited her list of reasons why Plug's upkeep would be so inexpensive, pointing out that Mr. Barnett had thrown in his tack for free, she finished by saying, "Why, when you come right down to it, we can hardly afford *not* to keep him!"

Her parents raised their eyebrows at that, but Cam was relieved to see that neither of them looked angry. In fact, she was pretty sure her father was trying hard not to smile. And she was delighted when Bonnie took her side.

"Personally, I think it's pretty neat," her sister said. "Cam's always wanted a horse, and now all of a sudden she's got one. I know it's not up to me, but if I had a vote I'd say let her keep him."

Cam gave Bonnie a grateful glance, then held her breath, waiting for her parents' verdict. It seemed to take forever before her mother spoke.

"I don't see why she shouldn't keep him," she said at last. "For the time being, anyway, until we see how it works out. What do you think, Hal?"

Cam's father nodded. "I'd go along with that." Turning to Cam, he added seriously, "But remember what your mother said – for the time being. This arrangement isn't necessarily permanent. If it turns out you can't control him, or if the animal makes the same kind of trouble for us that he did for Sam Barnett, I won't put up with it."

"Oh, he won't," Cam promised eagerly. "I won't let him! The only reason he kept getting into trouble was because nobody paid any attention to him. I'll be completely responsible for Plug. You and Mom won't have to worry about a single thing!"

"Well, honey, it looks like you've got yourself a horse," Mrs. Porter said, smiling.

"All right!" Cam sang out. She leaned down to give her mother a kiss, and then stood on tiptoe to kiss her father's cheek.

Bonnie grinned at her. "I guess now that you have a real horse you'll be joining the South Shore Centaurs, right?"

"Just as soon as I possibly can," Cam said happily. "But it'll probably take a few weeks for me to fix Plug up."

"You're not going to keep calling him Plug-Ugly, are you?" Bonnie asked. "In psychology class last semester, my professor said that weird nicknames can do a lot of damage to a person's ego. I wouldn't be surprised if it was the same with horses."

"Oh, no," Cam said "Like I told Nat, I'm definitely going to change his name. I just haven't decided yet what I'll call him. Maybe Lacey will have some good ideas. I'll call her right now. I can't wait to tell her I finally have my own horse, too!"

Bonnie stood up. "While you're doing that, I want to go out to the barn and take a look at the newest member of the family," she said. "Want to come with me, Mom?"

"Yes, indeed!" Mrs. Porter said. "A horse called Plug-Ugly has to be seen to be believed."

"When you see him, you'll believe it," Mr. Porter assured her.

Bonnie laughed. "Oh, come on, Dad. He can't really be *that* bad!"

41

"Well, he's no Moonracer, that's for sure," Cam said. "In fact, he's a total mess, but he won't be that way for long. When I'm through with him, Plug may not be gorgeous, but he'll look a lot better."

As her parents and Bonnie headed for the barn, Cam ran inside and picked up the phone in the hall. She was so excited that she dialed two wrong numbers before she finally reached her friend's house.

When Lacey answered, Cam didn't even say hello. "You'll never guess what happened today!" she cried.

"Cam? Is that you? What's up?"

"You've got to come out here right away! Is your mom there? Can she drive you?"

"Yeah, she's here. We just got back from Southampton a little while ago, and you would not *believe* how long it took us. The traffic on the Montauk was backed up for miles."

"I know all about it," Cam said, grinning. "So can you come?"

"Sure, I guess. Gee, Cam, you sound kind of weird. Is something wrong?" Lacey asked anxiously.

"Not wrong – terrific! Just get here as soon as you can okay?"

"I'm practically on my way. Cam, what's going on?" Lacey wailed. "I'm dying of curiosity! Can't you at least give me a hint?"

"Well … Okay, here goes." Cam grinned. "Do you think the South Shore Centaurs would have room for another member?" Then, right in the middle of Lacey's squeal of delight, she hung up and raced to the front porch to wait for her friend.

Although it seemed like an eternity, it was really less than fifteen minutes before Cam saw Mrs. Vining's car driving down the road. Even before it came to a complete stop in front of the house Lacey leaped out. Cam ran down the porch steps to meet her.

"Where is it?" Lacey cried as her mother drove off. *"What is it?"*

"What do you mean, what is it?" Cam said, laughing. "It's a horse, of course!"

"Believe it or not, I figured that out! I mean is it a stallion, a mare, or a gelding? How old is it? What color is it?"

"He's a gelding, he's about fourteen years old, he's brown, and he's in the barn," Cam told her.

Lacey threw her arms around Cam in a giant hug. "I'm so happy for you! Now we both have our own horses! So how did it happen? Where did he come from?"

"Remember that traffic jam you and your mom were caught in?" Lacey nodded. "Well, to make a long story short, there was this horse standing in the middle of the highway, I helped his owner get him off, and the man was so tired of chasing after him that he sold him to me for two cents."

"You're kidding! That is the most incredible thing I ever heard!" Lacey exclaimed. "You have to be the luckiest person in the entire world! Now let's see – the Centaurs are going on a trail ride next Thursday morning, so you can join then. Meet me at Seabreeze at nine o'clock, okay? And in the meantime whenever you're free, we can ride together, just the two of us! We're going to have so much fun!"

She grabbed Cam's hand. "Now come on. I can't wait to get a look at this horse." As they headed for the barn, Lacey added, "By the way, you haven't told me what his name is."

"That's not the only thing I haven't told you about him," Cam admitted. "To begin with, I'm not going to be able to ride him for a while."

Lacey frowned. "Uh-oh. I should have known there would be a catch, considering what you paid for him. What's the problem? Is he sick or lame or something?"

"More like 'or something,'" Cam said.

"What on earth –?" Lacey broke off when she saw Cam's mother and sister coming toward them. They both looked more than a little stunned. "Oh, hi, Mrs. Porter. Hi, Bonnie," Lacey said. "We're on our way to the barn to see Cam's horse."

Mrs. Porter smiled wanly. "It's quite a sight! We just came from there."

"Yeah," Bonnie said. "And you know something, Cam? Forget what I said about changing his name. Plug-Ugly suits him right down to the ground!"

Lacey stared after them as they passed. Turning back to Cam, she repeated, "Plug-Ugly? Exactly what's wrong with this horse of yours? Does it have two heads? Five legs? Three eyes?"

"Of course not! I don't know why everybody makes such a big deal out of the way he looks," Cam said crossly. "It's just that he's been out to pasture for a couple of years and he hasn't been groomed in ages. But if you'll help me, between the two of us we'll whip him into shape in no time."

"Why do I get the feeling this isn't going to be as easy as you make it sound?" Lacey muttered as she followed Cam into the barn.

FOUR

"WELL, HERE HE IS," CAM SAID TO LACEY, STOPPING in front of Plug's stall.

Somebody, her father, Cam guessed, had covered the floor with straw and tossed a pile of hay into one corner. The horse had been munching on the hay, but at the sound of her voice he lifted his shaggy head and glared suspiciously at Cam and Lacey.

"Oh, brother," Lacey breathed. "Bonnie wasn't kidding!"

"Use your imagination," Cam urged. "Try to picture him all washed and curried and brushed. Remember the ugly duckling that turned into a swan, and Beauty and the Beast, and Cinderella, and –"

Lacey groaned. "Cam, get real! Unless you have a fairy godmother you never told me about, there is no way you can turn that horse into a respectable mount, with or without my help!" More gently, she said, "Look, I don't want to burst your bubble, but if I ever saw a hopeless case, Plug-Ugly is it. If I were you, I'd return him to the guy you bought him from and get your two cents back."

Raising her chin defiantly, Cam said, "But you're not me! Okay, so Plug's not my dream horse. Speckles isn't

45

yours either, but I don't sneer at her just because she's a fat roan mare instead of a sleek black stallion!"

"Speckles is *not* fat!" Lacey objected. "She's solidly built, that's all! And I didn't sneer at Plug."

"You did too!"

"Did not!"

The girls scowled at each other, and then suddenly they both started to grin.

"Will you listen to us?" Lacey giggled. "We sound like we're eight years old instead of fourteen!"

"We sure do," Cam agreed. "Only, when we were eight years old, we didn't argue about our horses. They were absolutely perfect because they weren't real."

"Well, Speckles and Plug are real, all right," Lacey said, "and neither of them is perfect."

"That's for sure," Cam said ruefully, glancing at the brown gelding. "But until something better comes along, Plug-Ugly's all I've got and I'm not going to give him back. Will you help me fix him up? Please?"

Lacey smiled. "Yeah, sure. What are friends for? Besides, unless I give you a hand, we won't be able to ride together until *next* July!"

"Thanks, Lacey! I knew I could count on you," Cam said, beaming. "Let's go grab a sandwich, and then we'll get started." As they hurried back to the house, she went on, "The first thing we ought to do is comb all that junk out of Plug's mane and tail and give him a good currying to remove the dead hair. With both of us working we'll be done in no time flat. Then we can go to the beach with Nat and Ruthie. You can wear one of my bathing suits."

"Sounds like a great plan to me," Lacey replied. "On a broiling day like this, the ocean's going to feel fantastic!"

46

But two hours later Cam and Lacey were nowhere near the ocean. Drenched in sweat and covered with grime, they staggered out of Plug's stall and plopped down on the barn floor. Their arms ached from wielding the currycombs, and their noses and throats were clogged with the dust that rose in clouds from the gelding's furry hide.

"Where's that fairy godmother when you need her?" Lacey gasped when she had recovered from a coughing fit. She reached out and gingerly pressed one sneakered foot with her fingers. "Plug stepped on me so many times it's a wonder I have any toes left! What's more, I'm sure he did it on purpose. You'd think he'd be happy to get rid of that heavy winter coat, but instead he acted like we were trying to scalp him or something!"

"Yeah, I know." Cam sighed. "Plug doesn't know the meaning of the word *cooperate*. And the really awful part of it is that even though his mane and tail are in pretty good shape, the rest of him looks just the same!"

"Face it, Cam, we'll never be able to do this all by ourselves," Lacey said. "He needs clipping, and only a vet can do that. Better call Doc Connors first thing Monday morning. When he comes over, he can clip Plug, check him out, and give him his summer shots all at the same time."

"Shots?" Cam echoed. "Gosh, I forgot all about that."

"I did too until I got Speckles. Make-believe horses like Black Beauty and Moonracer never get sick, but *real* horses do," Lacey reminded her. "They're supposed to be vaccinated four times a year against all kinds of diseases – flu, tetanus, strangles, sleeping sickness, even rabies."

"Considering how long it must have been since Plug had any vet care at all, I guess he's pretty tough, not to mention lucky," Cam said.

Lacey nodded. "Better believe it. Oh, and when you talk to Doc, you ought to ask him for the name of a blacksmith. So far I've never had to use one for Speckles."

"I will. That's another thing make-believe horses don't need – shoes." Suddenly Cam felt a sharp tug on her scalp. *"Ouch*!" she squawked, whipping her head around to glare at the horse. "What do you think you're doing?"

Plug's neck was stretched out over his stall door and he had just taken a mouthful of her short blond hair, yanking at it with his teeth. When she slapped his nose, he snorted in disgust and turned away with an offended air.

Giggling, Lacey said, "I bet he thought your hair was hay – it's about the same color."

Just then Mr. Porter came into the barn. Seeing the girls sprawled on the floor, he put his hands on his hips and grinned down at them. "Your mother tells me you and Lacey have been beautifying Plug," he said to Cam. "I sure hope the horse looks better than you two do!"

Lacey groaned. "He doesn't, Mr. Porter." She stood up and held out a hand to Cam, pulling her to her feet.

"We gave up," Cam told her father. "We removed about half a ton of hair and there's at least another ton to go. Dr. Connors will have to clip him."

He peered at Plug. "Hmmm ... I'd say he's going to need a lot more than that. How about taking him to the barber for a real close shave?"

Cam made a face at him. "Very funny, Daddy."

She and Lacey made a feeble attempt to brush some of the dust from their shorts and shirts, which only made them start sneezing again.

"Bless you both," Mr. Porter said when they finally stopped. "I don't know what your plans are for the rest of

the afternoon, girls, but I have to go into town, so I thought
this might be a good time for Cam and me to go to the
Agway and pick up some feed for Plug. On the way, we
could drop you off at home, Lacey."

"Yes!" Lacey practically shouted. With an apologetic
glance at Cam, she added, "I know I said I'd help you, and
I did and I will, but I'm all sticky and itchy. I simply *have*
to get out of these filthy clothes and take a shower."

"I know how you feel," Cam said. "We're both pretty
grungy."

"That's putting it mildly," her father said. "Cam, you'd
better go back to the house and wash up a little, or they
won't let you into the store. I'll meet you and Lacey in a
few minutes."

As the girls started to follow Mr. Porter out of the barn,
Plug-Ugly stuck his head out of his stall and whinnied softly.

"Oh, Cam, look!" Lacey cried. "Isn't that cute? He
doesn't want you to go."

"That's only because he thinks I have a head full of
hay," Cam scoffed.

"Aren't you even going to say good-bye to him?"

Cam shrugged. "Sure." Without slowing her pace, she
called over her shoulder. "'Bye, horse. See you later."

"That's not what I meant," Lacey said, frowning. "Whenever
I leave Speckles, I always give her a treat and a big hug."

"Oh, come on, Lacey! That's totally different. You
really love Speckles. She's gentle, pretty sweet-tempered
– everything Plug's not."

"True. He's one of the least lovable animals I ever met,"
Lacey admitted. "But you said yourself he's all you've got,
and since you're determined to keep him, it wouldn't hurt
to be nice to him. You're all he's got, too, remember, and

49

it's not like Plug had a choice. By the way," she added, "you *are* going to change his name, aren't you?"

"Definitely," Cam said. "I just haven't had time to think about what to call him. Got any ideas?"

"How about Lucky?" Lacey suggested.

Cam shook her head. "Uh-uh. It has to be something really unusual, a name he can live up to."

"That's a pretty tall order. I'll work on it, though, and I'll call you if I think of anything."

"Do you think you can come out again tomorrow?" Cam asked.

"Afraid not. We're going to visit my grandparents in Sayville. But I'm sure I can come later in the week."

As soon as Cam had washed her face and hands, Mr. Porter drove the girls to Shorehaven in his big old station wagon.

"Thanks for everything, Lacey," Cam said as her friend got out in front of the Vinings' house. "I'm really sorry we never got to the beach."

"No problem," Lacey said. "The ocean will always be there, but it's not every day my best friend gets her own horse! I'll call tomorrow night when I get home to find out how you and Plug are getting along."

"Okay. And don't forget to think about a new name for him," Cam called as her father pulled away from the curb.

Their next stop was the Agway, where Cam and her father stocked up on sacks of grain and processed horse food. Cam also bought saddle soap and neat's-foot oil to use on Plug's tack.

"Remember, Daddy, I'm paying you back," Cam said as they pushed their loaded cart to the checkout counter.

The man behind the cash register grinned at Mr. Porter. "Afternoon, Hal. You buying all this stuff for Sam Barnett's horse?"

50

Cam and her father exchanged a startled glance. "Word sure travels fast around here," Mr. Porter said. "How did you find out about that, Fred?"

Fred's grin broadened. "Sam was in here just a little while ago, pleased as punch to get the animal off his hands. Said one of your girls paid two cents for him, and that's twice as much as a horse called Plug-Ugly is worth!" Chuckling to himself, Fred began ringing up the sale.

"Plug-Ugly! That's a good one!" said one of the other customers with a guffaw.

That did it. Cam saw red. She was hot, tired, and sick to death of hearing people make fun of Plug. After all, it wasn't his fault that he was such a mess, and since he was her horse now it was up to her to defend him.

Trying very hard to control her temper, she said, "Well, I'm the one who bought him, and I happen to think he's worth a lot more than two cents. And his name's not Plug-Ugly anymore," she added impulsively. "It's ..."

She glanced around at the displays of farm equipment, fertilizer, and feed sacks, searching for inspiration. Toro? Purina? Absorbine? Caterpillar? No, she couldn't possibly call Plug anything like that!

A poster advertising Galahad Tractors distracted Cam for a moment. *Imagine naming a tractor after a knight of King Arthur's Round Table*, she thought.

"Well, what is it, young lady?" Fred asked, still grinning. "What are you gonna call that horse?"

Cam spoke the first word that came into her head. "Galahad," she said, looking him straight in the eye. "His name is Galahad."

"*Galahad*?" At Lacey's incredulous screech, Cam winced and held the receiver away from her ear. Lacey had called

51

on Sunday night as she had promised and Cam had just told her Plug's new name. "As in Sir Galahad, the pure and perfect knight? Oh, wow! That's something to live up to, all right!"

"I don't see what's wrong with it," Cam said a little huffily. "It's a pretty dumb name for a tractor, but I don't see what's wrong with it for a horse."

"Well, it sure beats Plug-Ugly by a mile," Lacey admitted. "So how's Plug – I mean, Galahad – doing?"

"Not bad. Pretty good, in fact. I talked Nate and Bonnie into helping me give him a bath this morning," Cam told her. "It took forever, but we had the afternoon shift at the stand, so there was plenty of time."

"You're kidding! Where'd you find a tub big enough?"

"Not in a tub, dummy. It was more like a shower. I tied Galahad outside the barn, and then we turned the hose on him. We used all of Bonnie's wildflower shampoo, and after Nate rinsed him off, we let him dry in the sun. Naturally, Galahad hated it and he made a terrible fuss. He still looks awfully scruffy, but at least now he's clean, and he smells great."

Lacey giggled. "Gee, I miss all the fun! I can hardly wait to smell him. But I'm afraid I'll have to, because I just found out I'll be helping Dad at the store all next week. One of the kids who works for him broke his collarbone bodysurfing over the weekend, so I'm filling in until he can hire a replacement."

"Bummer," Cam said sympathetically. "I guess that means you'll miss the Centaurs' trail ride on Thursday, too."

"Yeah. But most of all I'll miss Speckles, and she'll miss me. She goes off her feed if I don't visit her every day. And don't you dare tell me she could stand to lose weight!"

"I didn't really mean what I said about her being fat," Cam said. "Come when you can, and I'll keep you posted on what's happening with Galahad. I'm going to call Doc Connors first thing in the morning. The next time you see him, I bet you won't even recognize him – Galahad I mean, not the vet!"

After they hung up Cam said goodnight to her parents, scooped up Jupiter, and carried him to her room. She showered, brushed her teeth, and turned on the electric fan on her windowsill. Then she moved the protesting cat from his favorite spot on her pillow and flopped down on her bed, gazing at the picture of Moonracer.

"Now that Lacey's got Speckles, she's given up on the dream we had when we were kids, but I haven't," Cam told the while stallion. "Plug – oops, Galahad – is just my *first* horse, not the only one I'll ever own. After he's back in shape and I've been riding with the Centaurs for a while, maybe I'll try to sell him. I bet the people at Stonyfield Stables where Lacey and I took riding lessons would buy him. Then I could get a much nicer horse. I'll keep trading up until I have a beautiful, perfect horse just like you ..."

Yawning, Cam turned out her bedside lamp. Lulled by the gentle whirring of the fan, she dozed off and slipped into a dream she'd had many times before. At least, it started out that way.

She and Lacey were riding Moonracer and Black Beauty across a green, grassy paddock. The white horse and the black galloped side by side, flying faster than the wind, and the rhythmic drumming of their hooves echoed the beat of Cam's happily pounding heart. That's when the dream changed. Lacey's horse began pulling ahead, only he wasn't a sleek black stallion anymore. He had turned into a plump roan mare.

"Lacey, where are you going? Wait for me!" Cam shouted, but Speckles didn't slow her pace. All of a sudden Cam heard the sound of hoofbeats approaching from behind.

"Look, Cam! Look back," Lacey called over her shoulder. "It's Galahad. He doesn't want you to leave!"

Cam turned in her saddle. Moonracer seemed to be galloping in slow motion now, and to her dismay she saw a horse gaining on them. It was Galahad, all right, but there was something very strange about him. As he got closer, Cam realized that instead of his shaggy brown coat he was covered with wildflowers.

"What are you doing here?" she yelled. "Stop following me! Shoo! Go away! Get lost!"

The sound of her own voice woke her, and Cam sat bolt upright in bed. "It's not fair," she muttered. "That was such a terrific dream until Galahad showed up and ruined everything. I sure hope he's not going to make a habit of it!" Turning her pillow over to the cool side, Cam lay back down and soon drifted off into a deep and dreamless sleep.

She was awakened again shortly before dawn by a thunderclap that almost jolted both her and Jupiter right out of bed. Cam barely had time to take the fan off her windowsill and pull down the sash before the rain started coming down in torrents.

"The last thing we need is another storm," she said to the cat. "If this keeps up, our tomatoes are going to rot right off the vines and the raspberries will get all mushy."

Later that morning, after Cam had slogged through the rain to feed and water her horse, she made an appointment with the vet for the following afternoon. Next she phoned the blacksmith Doc Connors had recommended and arranged for him to trim Galahad's hooves and shoe him on Thursday.

For most of the day Cam helped her family with chores around the house. Then she went out to the barn to start cleaning Galahad's tack.

"Remember what this is?" she asked, holding the bridle up in front of the gelding's nose. He sniffed at it suspiciously, then gave his head a vigorous shake and turned away with a snort.

Cam couldn't help grinning. "Oh, you do too! You're just playing dumb. And if you have forgotten, I'll teach you."

Galahad stamped and flicked his ears as if her voice were an annoying fly. "Yeah, I know. You don't like that idea. But you'd better get used to it, because I'm going to turn you into a decent saddle horse whether you like it or not. After Doc Connors and the blacksmith are through with you, we'll have our first lesson – maybe even this weekend."

FIVE

DR. CONNORS WAS A BLUFF, HEARTY IRISHMAN in his late sixties who had taken care of the Porters' dog and cats for many years. When he examined Galahad on Tuesday afternoon, he discovered that in addition to suffering from malnutrition, the gelding had an infection in all four feet, plus a skin condition Doc called "rain scald." According to the vet, all Galahad's problems were the result of his being kept in a damp, muddy pasture without shelter, proper nourishment, or grooming for so long.

"I can't understand it," he muttered, shaking his gray head. "Sam Barnett treats his pigs and cows like royalty, but this poor creature … Well, it's a crying shame, that's what it is. I know it's hard to believe, Cambria, but only a few years ago this was a fine-looking horse. Not a beauty, mind you, but spirited and strong."

He patted Cam on the shoulder. "And he will be again, never fear. With you to look after him, he'll soon get the sparkle back in his eye and the spring in his step. Tender loving care is the best medicine for an ailing animal, and I'm sure you'll give it to him. They say there's nothing like the bond between a boy and his dog, but in my experience it comes in a poor second to the love of a girl for her horse."

Cam didn't want him to get the wrong impression. "That's not the way it is with Galahad and me. Doc," she said. "I feel sorry or him, but I don't love him. I guess you might say he's kind of a *temporary horse*."

The vet looked puzzled. "A temporary horse? I don't think I've ever heard that term before."

"Well, I've always wanted a horse, but Galahad's not the horse I've always wanted, so I won't be keeping him forever," Cam explained. "You see, when my friend Lacey Vining got Speckles, she joined a riding club, but I couldn't because I didn't have a horse. And then I found Galahad, and even though he wasn't my dream horse, he was practically free …"

"Ah, I'm beginning to understand," Dr. Connors interrupted. "You want to ride with Lacey and the South Shore Centaurs, and any horse is better than no horse at all, correct?"

Cam nodded. "That's it exactly. But while he's mine, I'll take good care of him, Doc. Just tell me what to do."

"I will indeed," the vet said. "But I'm warning you, my girl, you won't have an easy time of it."

He rolled up his sleeves and set to work. After he gave Galahad his shots and clipped him, he showed Cam how to rub ointment on the sore places on the gelding's back and sides that had been hidden by his long hair. Cam was shocked to see how many of them there were.

No wonder he acted the way he did when Lacey and I were currying him, she thought, feeling a stab of guilt. *It must have hurt an awful lot*!

She watched intently as Dr. Connors cleaned each of Galahad's hooves and packed them with antibiotic powder. He told Cam that his assistant, Dr. Marx, would come out once a day for the rest of the week to repeat the procedure.

57

Then he outlined Cam's tasks. She would have to change Galahad's bedding morning and evening so that the straw was always clean and dry, bathe him regularly with a special antiseptic shampoo to clear up his skin problems, and groom him each day using only a soft brush and polishing cloth. She was to follow the feeding schedule the vet wrote down, adding the vitamin supplements he prescribed, and make sure that the horse had plenty of fresh water to drink.

Doc also gave Cam a list of things she would need to buy for Galahad. Her eyes widened when she saw how many there were – the shampoo, the vitamins, insect repellent, liniment and antiseptic ointment, plus a soft pad to place under the saddle when she began to ride him. Cam was beginning to realize that taking proper care of her horse wasn't going to be as simple – or as inexpensive – as she had thought.

"Galahad's general health will improve dramatically, and so will his feet once they're properly trimmed and shod," Doc said. "Did you call the blacksmith I recommended?"

"Yes. He's coming Thursday morning."

"Good. Joe Maxwell's the best in the business. You can be sure he'll do a fine job." Giving the gelding a brisk pat, Doc left the stall. He went over to the tap near the barn door, and as he scrubbed his hands, using the antiseptic soap he'd brought with him, he said, "Unless something goes wrong, which I doubt it will, your 'temporary' horse will be fit as a fiddle by mid-August at the very latest."

Cam couldn't hide her disappointment. "The middle of August? Not until then?"

"I'm afraid not. I know how eager you are to ride

him, Cambria, but Galahad needs plenty of rest and recuperation. He's had a hard life over the past couple of years, poor fellow. It'll take a while before he feels like himself again."

The vet put on his raincoat and picked up his black bag. "Well, I'll be going now. I've a number of other patients to see. Dr. Marx will come out tomorrow at around the same time to medicate Galahad's hooves, and I'll be dropping by to give him a thorough checkup once a week until I'm satisfied that he's completely recovered."

Cam walked with him to the door. "Uh, Doc, could you give me some idea of what his treatment is going to cost?" she asked.

"You needn't worry about that, Cambria. I'll send my bill to your father," he said. "I'll just add it to the balance he owes for Sailor's last checkup."

"Oh, no, please don't," Cam said quickly. "Send it to me. I'm paying for all Galahad's expenses myself."

Dr. Connors looked surprised. "You are, are you? Very commendable, I'm sure. That's what I'll do then. Give my regards to your family – and Sailor and the cats, of course." He fished a crumpled tweed hat out of his raincoat pocket and jammed it on his head. "Dreadful weather, isn't it? Rainiest summer I can remember since I left Ireland twenty years ago." He mumbled as he splashed through the puddles to his car.

The *middle* of August, Cam thought with a sigh. *That's almost four more weeks, and who knows how much longer it'll take for Galahad to get used to the saddle and bridle again? At this rate, I won't be riding with Lacey and the Centaurs until Christmas!*

She wandered back to Galahad's stall and leaned over

59

the door, watching him gobble great mouthfuls of hay. He certainly didn't look any better. If anything, he looked even worse now that he had been clipped. His brown coat was dull, and without all that shaggy hair, Cam could clearly see his sores and how thin he was.

"Mr. Barnett ought to be put in jail for letting you get this way," she muttered. "I sure can't blame you for running away from him!"

Galahad gave her a quick, walleyed glance and kept on chomping.

"That's right – eat as much as you want. Nobody's going to take it away from you, and there's plenty more where that came from. All you have to do is what Doc Connors said – eat, rest and get well."

Over the next several weeks, Galahad followed the doctor's orders to the letter. So did Cam, and she soon learned what the vet meant when he said she wouldn't have an easy time of it. What with tending to her horse, doing her regular chores around the farm, and taking her turn at the roadside stand, she had never worked harder in her life. But it was worth it, because every day Galahad's health and appearance improved just as Dr. Connors had promised.

The gelding's ribs and prominent hipbones were gradually disappearing beneath a layer of fat. Thanks to Cam's careful grooming, his coat was developing a glossy sheen. The sores on his back and sides were healing nicely, and so were his newly shod hooves. Even the most skeptical members of Cam's family had to admit that there might be hope for her two-cent horse after all.

The change in him was particularly apparent to Lacey, who saw him only once or twice a week. She wasn't able to come to the farm more often because her father had asked her to stay on at the store for the rest of the summer as a part-time replacement for Sean.

"He doesn't want to hire anybody full-time because business hasn't been so great lately," Lacey told Cam. "Dad's even laid off a couple of people. All this rain we've been having has really cut down on sales of seasonal stuff. People just aren't buying things like boogie boards, beach umbrellas, and barbecue grills."

Fortunately, August made up for a soggy July by being unusually hot and dry. At Doc Connor's third weekly visit, he told Cam that she could begin walking Galahad outside on a lead. When she brought the gelding out of the barn a few days later, he tossed his head and kicked up his heels like a colt, delighted to be released from his stall. Cam was surprised to see that in the bright sunlight his coat was a rich chestnut shade instead of plain ordinary brown.

Her father and Ruthie were watching while she led Galahad around the barnyard at a brisk jog. "Now, that's a horse of a different color," Mr. Porter joked.

From her perch on top of the fence, Ruthie said, "I'm glad Galahad isn't ugly anymore. How much longer till you'll be able to ride him, Cam?"

"Just a couple more weeks."

"Will you let me ride him sometimes?" Ruthie asked eagerly. "Not right away, but after he's busted."

Cam and Mr. Porter both laughed. "He *was* busted, but now he's almost fixed!" Cam teased.

Ruthie frowned. "You know what I mean. Bronco-busting, like the cowboys do."

"Galahad's not a wild mustang, Ruthie." Cam led him over to the fence. "He's not wild at all. He's just a horse that hasn't been ridden in a long time. A middle-aged

61

horse," she added, knowing their father's concern for her safety. "He's feeling frisky because he's been cooped up for so long, but now that he'll be getting regular exercise he'll calm down in a hurry."

"I certainly hope so," Mr. Porter said as Galahad pawed the ground and did what looked like an impatient little dance step.

"Then if he doesn't have to be busted, will you let me ride him?" Ruthie persisted.

Cam shrugged. "Maybe. We'll see."

"You sound just like Mom and Daddy!" Ruthie moaned. "That's what they always say whenever I want to do anything fun. I *hate* being the youngest!"

"Stop bugging your sister, honey," Mr. Porter said firmly. "Nobody's going to be riding Galahad for a while yet, including Cam. I also don't look forward to worrying about two of my daughters breaking their necks. At least Cam knows how to ride, but you've never been on a horse in your life."

Ruthie stuck out her lower lip. "I have so! Last year at the Fishermen's Fair they had a pony, and I rode him lots and lots."

"Sitting on a pony while somebody leads it around in a circle isn't the same as riding a horse all by yourself," Cam pointed out. "Let's talk about this later, okay? I'm supposed to be exercising Galahad, but all we're doing is standing here."

"Oh, okay, I guess. Can I give him this first?" Ruthie took a sugar lump out of a pocket of her shorts. "I saved it specially for him."

Galahad pricked up his ears and stretched out his neck, but Cam held him back.

"Better not," she said. "Doc told me exactly what to feed him, and he didn't say anything about sugar. I know it's bad for Galahad's teeth, and it might upset his digestion."

Ruthie promptly dug into her other pocket and pulled out a carrot. "Then how about this?"

Cam grabbed Galahad's halter before he could snatch the carrot from her sister's hand. "They're not on his diet either. Besides, I don't want to spoil him. He shouldn't have any treats until he's earned them."

Galahad watched wistfully as Ruthie took a bite of the carrot herself. "Poor Galahad!" she sighed. "If he was *my* horse, I wouldn't be so mean to him."

"Cam's not being mean, honey. She's just being strict," their father said. "That's not the same thing."

"Galahad has to learn who's in charge, or I'll never be able to train him," Cam explained. "And if I can't do that, I won't be able to ride him and neither will you – if I decide to let you, that is."

"When you start training him, can I watch?" Ruthie asked.

Cam's patience was wearing thin. "No! You'll just disturb his concentration." Tugging on the lead line, she said to the horse, "Come on, lazybones. You've rested long enough. Let's get moving!"

The long-awaited day finally came when Doc Connors told Cam she could begin riding Galahad. The vet arrived late on a Monday afternoon. After examining the gelding one last time, Doc told Cam she had done an excellent job of caring for Galahad and gave him a clean bill of health. He also gave Cam the bill for his services.

"I took you at your word, Cambria," the vet said as he handed her the envelope. "I'm sure you won't be able to pay this all at once, and I don't expect you to. Take all the

63

time you need. You might want to call Mrs. Grayson, my receptionist, sometime in September. She'll be happy to help you arrange an installment plan."

Cam had known all along that all the care Doc Connors had given Galahad wouldn't come cheap, and now she was almost afraid to look at his bill. She waited until he had driven away before taking it out of the envelope. Even though she thought she was prepared, when Cam saw the amount her jaw dropped.

"One thousand dollars! Holy cow!" she gasped, sinking down onto a bale of straw. "I'm only fourteen years old, and I'm a thousand dollars in debt. By the time I pay this off, I'll be an old lady and Doc will probably be *dead*!"

Over the past four weeks Cam's savings had melted away, and her allowance seemed to disappear as if by magic. The blacksmith had expected to be paid in cash when his job was done, and as Cam had counted out the bills she doubted her parents spent that much on shoes for the whole family. The items on Doc's list had turned out to be even more expensive than she'd feared. Also, she now knew from personal experience what "eating like a horse" meant. Galahad was a bottomless pit, and Cam was sure she must be one of the Agway's best customers. Although she hated to do it, she had been forced to charge his feed and supplies to her father, promising to pay him back as soon as she could. And now there was Doc Connors' bill.

Cam turned to stare at Galahad. Galahad stared back. He was swinging his head from side to side and shifting his weight from one foot to another – weaving, the vet called it. Now that the gelding was feeling fit again and Cam had started exercising him, he was always bored and restless whenever he was shut up in his stall.

"I don't believe this," she mumbled, still in a mild state of shock. "For what you're costing me, I could buy a Thoroughbred!"

Galahad snorted in disdain and shook himself all over as if he were telling Cam exactly what he thought of Thoroughbreds. She might have been amused if she hadn't been so stunned. Shoving Doc's bill into a pocket of her jeans, she trudged back to the house for supper.

Cam had no appetite that night. While her family sat around the big old table in the dining room, wolfing down corn on the cob, fried chicken, hot biscuits, and tons of salad, she picked at her food hoping no one would notice how little she was eating. Lost in her worries, Cam didn't feel much like talking, either, so she answered everybody's questions about Dr. Connors' final visit as briefly as she could.

After supper, her parents and Bonnie took their coffee out onto the screened porch and Scott and Nathan drove off to a softball game in Scott's clunker. Cam, Natalie, and Ruthie were on kitchen detail. As they cleared the table, Natalie said, "Cam, is anything the matter? You're awfully quiet, and you hardly ate a thing."

"Doc didn't find something wrong with Galahad that you didn't tell us about, did he?" Ruthie asked anxiously.

Cam forced a smile. "Oh, no. Galahad's perfectly fine. I guess I'm just tired, that's all."

"No wonder," Natalie said. "I've got to hand it to you, Cam. You've really knocked yourself out taking care of that horse, and it shows. When I first saw him that day at the stand back when he was still Plug-Ugly, I thought you were nuts for wasting even two cents on him, but I have to admit I was wrong."

65

"Me too," Ruthie agreed. "Even with his funny eye, Galahad's worth a whole lot more than that now!"

"You can say that again," Cam said with a hollow laugh. "You wouldn't believe how much more!"

As soon as she and her sisters had finished loading the dishwasher and cleaning up the kitchen, Cam raced upstairs to share her problem with Lacey. She didn't want anyone listening in, so she used the phone in her parents' bedroom.

"What am I going to do?" she wailed after she told her friend about Doc Connors's humongous bill. "The only installment plan I could possibly afford would be a payment a month for the next ten years! Doc said to take my time, but I'm pretty sure that's not the kind of time he had in mind."

"You could always ask your folks to help out," Lacey suggested.

"No way! I've already had to charge some of Galahad's stuff to Daddy, even though I promised I'd pay all his expenses myself."

"Yeah, but that was before you found out how expensive he was going to be."

"You might have warned me, you know," Cam said accusingly. "After all, you're the one with horse experience."

"But I'm not the one who pays Speckles's bills. Dad takes care of all that," Lacey reminded her. "Look, Cam, you don't have to pay anything until next month, so why get all bent out of shape about it now? They don't throw people into debtors' prison anymore, you know. If you want my advice, I'd say save up as much of your allowance as you can from now on, and work out a payment schedule in September like Doc said."

Cam was beginning to feel a little less frantic. "I guess you're right. Galahad's shoes are paid for, and I just bought enough feed to see him through October. Unless some other major expenses crop up, I ought to be able to save quite a bit. And who knows? Maybe I'll win a lottery or something before then …"

"Hey, anything's possible," Lacey said cheerfully. "Now that that's settled, let's talk about fun stuff. When are you going to start riding Galahad?"

"Tomorrow morning," Cam said. "I've got the afternoon shift at the stand, so that'll give me a couple of hours to work with him. I've been bridling him every day for the past week to get him used to the bit, and yesterday and today I put the saddle on him. Galahad blew himself up so I couldn't fasten the girth, but when I poked him in the belly he deflated like a pricked balloon."

Lacey giggled. "I'm working at the store tomorrow and Wednesday, but maybe I can ride over later in the week. Then I can introduce Speckles to Galahad. The two of them ought to get acquainted before we start riding together. Wouldn't it be neat if they became best friends like we are?"

Cam thought about that for a moment. "I'm not so sure it would," she said.

"Why not?" Lacey asked, surprised.

"Because if they really started to like each other, Speckles would probably miss Galahad when I sell him."

"You're still planning to do that, huh? I thought maybe now that you've spent so much time with him, you might have changed your mind."

"Nope, Galahad's just my first stop on the way to my dream horse," Cam said. "Anyway, while I'm training him, I'll need his undivided attention, and Speckles would only distract him."

Lacey sighed. "I guess maybe she would. I never thought about that. Okay, we won't come over right away, but I'll call you tomorrow night to find out how the first session goes."

The girls had said their good-byes and were about to hang up when Lacey exclaimed, "Oh, Cam, wait! I almost forgot! On the Saturday before Labor Day the Centaurs are having a sunset trail ride and a cookout on the beach. It was supposed to be a clambake, but all the parents said that was too expensive, so we're just having hamburgers and hot dogs. It'll be a real end-of-summer blast. If Galahad's ready by then, do you think your folks will let you go?"

"I'm sure they will," Cam said happily. "Galahad will be ready, or else! Can I bring dessert or something?"

"How about one of your mom's fabulous pies?" Lacey suggested. "On second thought, better make that two – there'll be nine of us, counting you. Dad will be taking all the food to the beach in the Jeep, so he could swing by your place on the way and pick them up."

Cam was so excited at the prospect of her first outing with the South Shore Centaurs that she had a hard time falling asleep that night. When she finally did, her dreams were jumbled and strange. In the strangest one of all, she was cantering along the seashore with Lacey and the other girls in the club, but they weren't riding their horses. From the waist down, they *were* horses! They had turned into centaurs, the mythical creatures for whom the club was named.

Everybody except Cam seemed to be having a wonderful time, but then, nobody except Cam was having trouble with her bottom half. If she tried to keep pace with the others, the horse half of her body lagged behind. If she

68

wanted to go left, it swerved to the right. Then it started cantering in reverse, and Cam lost her temper.

"Moonracer, what's the matter with you? I'm supposed to be in charge here!" she shouted. But when she turned around to glare at the disobedient part of her, Cam saw that it was glossy chestnut, not milky white. "Galahad!" she groaned. "I might have known! How am I ever going to train you if you won't do what I tell you?"

Ruthie suddenly appeared on a pony that Mr. Porter was leading. "See how well I can ride?" she called to Cam, waving a fistful of carrots. Cam tried to grab a carrot, but Ruthie shook her head sadly. "Sorry – they're not on your diet."

"Don't be so mean," Cam wailed. "I'm awfully hungry …"

She broke off when she heard a deep rumbling noise.

"Thunderstorm!" her father yelled. "Run for cover!"

As Cam opened her eyes, she realized that the rumbling was coming from her stomach.

"What a crazy dream! That'll teach me to go to bed without any supper!" she muttered. But just in case she was still asleep, she peeked under the sheet to make sure nothing was there but her own two legs.

SIX

AFTER BREAKFAST, FORTIFIED WITH ENOUGH pacakes and sausage to see her through the morning, Cam helped Bonnie sort and wash the beach plums Natalie and Nathan had picked for the jam their mother was going to make. As soon as she was finished she raced to the barn, where she mucked out Galahad's stall and fed him. She groomed him even more thoroughly than usual, combing his mane and tail and polishing his coat until it shone like fine mahogany.

"This is it, Galahad. Today's the big day," Cam told the horse as she brought his tack into the stall.

Galahad didn't seem at all impressed. As usual, he puffed himself up when she put the saddle on his back, and as usual Cam gave him a poke. With an irritable snort and a stamp or two, Galahad deflated, reluctantly, allowing her to fasten the girth. He wasn't any happier about being bridled, but weeks of practice had made Cam adept at getting the bit into his mouth. Then, settling her helmet firmly on her head she led the gelding outside.

Cam was surprised and not particularly pleased to find her father and Scott there, tinkering with the tractor. She planned to ride Galahad around the barnyard today, and as she had made clear to everyone in her family, the last thing she wanted was an audience.

"Looking good, honey," Mr. Porter said with a smile.

Cam frowned. "Are you two going to be here very long?"

"It depends," Scott replied vaguely.

"On what?"

"On how long it takes to find out what's wrong with this machine," their father said. "Don't mind us, honey. You go right ahead and give Galahad his lesson."

"Yeah, Cam," Scott added. "And if he throws you, we can get you to the hospital in fifteen minutes – Dad clocked it the other day. Mom made us bring a first-aid kit, too. It's on the tractor seat."

"And I bet there's an ambulance parked around the side of the barn!" Cam sighed. "Oh, Daddy, I told you nothing like that is going to happen. Doesn't anybody in this family have any faith in me?"

"Hey, I'm not worried. If you break your neck, I've still got three more sisters," Scott joked.

"Your mother and I have all the faith in the world in you. It's *him* we're not so sure of," Mr. Porter said, indicating the gelding with a jerk of his head. Galahad gazed at him mildly, the very picture of walleyed innocence.

"So are you going to try to ride him or what?" Scott asked.

Cam glared at her brother. "For your information, I am not going to *try* to ride him, I am going to ride him. And I'd appreciate it if you and Daddy would just fix the tractor – if there's really something wrong with it, that is – instead of baby-sitting Galahad and me. We can manage perfectly fine on our own!"

With that, she gathered up the reins and put her foot in the stirrup, intending to spring gracefully into the saddle.

Galahad, however, was a fairly tall horse and Cam was not a very tall girl. Also, there was no mounting block. After a couple of awkward scrambles, red-faced with embarrassment, she muttered, "Would somebody please give me a leg up?"

"Sure – no problem," Scott said with a grin as he boosted her onto the gelding's back.

The minute Galahad felt Cam's weight he skittered sideways, almost unseating her. But she quickly slipped her right foot into the other stirrup and gripped him with her legs while she pulled back on the reins. Galahad didn't like that at all. Flattening his ears, he kicked a couple of times.

"Ride 'em, cowgirl!" Scott shouted. At the same time Mr. Porter called out, "Cam, be careful!"

More shaken than she would ever admit, Cam ignored them both. All her attention was focused on her horse. "Oh, no you don't!" she said between clenched teeth, shortening the reins even more. Trying to escape the pressure, Galahad began to back up.

Just like in that crazy dream, Cam thought. Aloud, she said, "You want to play games? That's okay with me. You won't get very far, though, because you're about to run into –" the gelding's hindquarters hit the side of the barn with a solid thump – "a wall!"

Startled by the impact, Galahad snorted indignantly and leaped forward. He would have broken into a gallop if Cam hadn't hauled on the reins with all her strength. By now she realized that Galahad not only had a mind of his own but also a mouth of iron and she was grateful that his bridle had a curb bit that was all in one piece. With a snaffle, two pieces of metal linked together, she would never have been able to control him.

Holding the horse to a prancing, lunging gait somewhere between a bone-jarring trot and a teeth-rattling canter, Cam managed to guide him through the open gateway into the barnyard. Her father and Scott had stopped pretending to work on the tractor and were hanging over the fence, watching her every move.

"Shut the gate!" Cam yelled to them over her shoulder and Scott quickly did.

As Galahad charged across the yard, she leaned back, sawing on the reins. Although the gelding fought her every step of the way, he finally settled into something like a normal trot, but his gait was so uneven that Cam found it impossible to post gently and rhythmically the way she had been taught. Every time her bottom hit the saddle it felt as if her spine were about to jab right into her skull. With each jounce her stomach lurched, making her wish she hadn't eaten such a big breakfast.

I bet Galahad knows it, too, she thought grimly. *I'm sure he's doing this on purpose!*

After they had circled the barnyard several more times, she dragged him to a walk. Both horse and rider were drenched in sweat. Cam's arms, legs, and shoulders ached, and her head was pounding. She also felt a little queasy, but she had a proud grin on her face as she stopped Galahad in front of her father and brother.

"Well, I guess I showed him who's boss!" she said.

"I guess you did," Mr. Porter agreed. He was smiling too, but Cam thought he looked a little pale, in spite of his tan.

Scott reached over to give Galahad a pat.

"Pretty impressive, kid. I didn't know you had it in you. What happens next?"

73

"I'm going to walk him for a while," Cam told him. "Then, after we've both cooled off a little, we'll trot some more. I don't want to try a canter for a few more days." She nudged Galahad with her heels and made a crisp clucking sound.

He didn't move a muscle.

She nudged him harder. "Let's go!"

Galahad paid no attention. He just stuck his head through the fence rails and tried to grab a bite of the weeds outside.

Jerking on the reins, Cam said, "*Galahad*! Listen up! I'm talking to you!"

The horse flicked his ears, raised one hind foot, and scratched at his belly with it.

"Looks like Galahad has his own ideas," Scott said.

Cam brushed away the sweat that was trickling down her face from under her helmet. "Too bad! He has to realize that I'm in charge here, not him." She slapped the gelding's rump. "Get a move on, horse!"

Galahad stayed where he was.

Hot, achy, and frustrated, Cam flapped the reins on the horse's neck, digging her heels into his sides as hard as she could. "Galahad, *walk*!" she commanded.

He didn't.

"I've got jumper cables in my car. Want me to try jump-starting him?" Scott offered with a grin.

"Why don't you call it a day, Cam?" Their father suggested. "It seems that Galahad's had enough lessons for one morning, and I think maybe you have too."

"The only lesson I've learned is that this horse is every bit as stubborn as Mr. Barnett said he was," she said. "But he'll find out that I can be stubborn, too. I'll make him walk if it's the last thing I ever – Hey! Where do you think you're going?"

74

Galahad had suddenly lunged forward, almost jolting Cam out of the saddle, and now he took off across the barnyard at a lurching canter. Pulling back on the reins, she yelled. "*Whoa!* I said *walk*! Don't you understand English?"

To Cam's surprise, it didn't take long at all to slow the gelding down. In fact, he obeyed so quickly and walked so sedately that she was suspicious.

"You seem awfully pleased with yourself. Got any more tricks up your sleeve?"

As if in answer to her question, Galahad flicked his ears and shook his head vigorously.

"Good! I admit you caught me off guard that time, but believe me, it won't happen again," Cam promised. "And if you think that little demonstration proves you're the boss of this outfit, you're wrong." She nudged him sharply with her heels. "Now, let's trot!"

Cam arranged her schedule at the farm stand for the next two weeks so she could work afternoons and train Galahad in the mornings before it got too hot. Every day she walked and trotted him in the pasture behind the barn, but neither Cam nor Galahad enjoyed their lessons. Although Galahad had given up trying to unseat her, it was a constant struggle to make him obey her commands. He fought the bit, and when all else failed he switched into the stop-and-start mode that drove Cam crazy. From beginning to end, each session was a battle of wills, and at the end of it Cam was never quite sure who won.

The gelding's behavior wasn't any better in his stall. He nipped at Cam when she groomed or saddled him, chewed on his feed box and the top of the wooden door, and kicked the walls. Hoping that more freedom might help Galahad's disposition she started letting him out into the pasture at night. Unfortunately, Cam didn't latch the gate securely on Thursday, and while everyone was sound asleep Galahad managed to escape. Cam's parents were less than thrilled when they found him the following morning in the middle of Mrs. Porter's trampled flowerbeds, feasting on her prized zinnias and asters.

"I don't know what to do with him. He's absolutely impossible!" Cam told Lacey on the phone later that day. "The Centaurs cookout is a week from tomorrow, and I can't see that I've made any progress at all. Will you please come out here? Maybe you can give me some pointers."

"I guess I could." Lacey said. "But would you mind if I rode over on Speckles? I know you said you'd rather I didn't but I haven't taken her out since Tuesday and she really needs the exercise."

"I don't care if you're riding Godzilla! Just come," Cam begged. "I'm in big trouble here!"

When Lacey and Speckles arrived early Friday morning, Cam had already been battling with Galahad in the pasture for about half an hour. She was concentrating so hard on forcing him into a steady trot, she didn't even notice them until Galahad did. At the sight of Speckles he raised his head and pricked up his ears, whickering a greeting. The mare whickered back and Lacey waved to Cam.

"I don't know what you're complaining about," she said as she dismounted and looped Speckle's reins around a fence rail. "Galahad looks great!"

"Well, appearances can be deceiving," Cam said softly. "His outside may be in good shape, but inside he's still Plug-Ugly."

She turned the gelding toward the fence. Much to her surprise, he didn't give her the usual argument. Instead he trotted right over to where Speckles stood. The two horses touched noses, whuffing softly.

Lacey grinned. "Hey, will you look at that," she exclaimed. "They like each other!"

Cam twitched the reins. "That's enough schmoozing," she told Galahad. "We've got a lot of work to do today. Watch us now, Lacey. I'm going to put him through his paces – or try to, anyway – and I want you to tell me if I'm doing something wrong."

She clucked to the gelding, prodding him with her heels. Although he reluctantly began to walk, he kept turning his head to look back at Speckles. She whinnied, and Galahad whinnied in reply.

"Stop that!" Cam ordered with a sharp jerk on the reins. "You're supposed to be paying attention to me, not her."

Leaning forward slightly in the saddle, she did her best to make him trot, but Galahad just plodded along, never taking his eyes from the other horse.

This was a really dumb idea. I shouldn't have told Lacey she could bring Speckles today, Cam thought, becoming more frustrated by the minute. *I knew she'd distract him and that's exactly what she's doing.*

Finally, when they were halfway around the pasture, Galahad picked up his pace. Arching his neck and tossing his head, he trotted briskly until he reached Speckles again. Then he came to a sudden halt, and no matter how hard Cam tried he refused to budge.

"See what I mean?" she said to Lacey in disgust as Galahad and Speckles snorted and snuffled at each other. "He does that all the time! I never used to believe in using a crop on a horse, but now I'm not so sure. Do you think if I gave him a couple of good whacks, he'd get the message?"

Lacey didn't reply. Leaning over the fence, she stroked Galahad's glossy neck.

"Well, do you?" Cam persisted.

"No, I don't," Lacey said at last. "You asked me to tell you if you were doing anything wrong, so here goes." Taking a deep breath, she looked Cam straight in the eye. "I'm certainly no expert, but it seems to me you've been doing *everything* wrong from the day you brought Galahad home."

Cam couldn't have been more shocked and hurt if her best friend had slapped her in the face.

Before she could gather her wits to protest, Lacey went on. "Look, Cam, I know Galahad's just a substitute for the perfect horse of your dreams, and he'll never be as beautiful as that picture you have hanging on your wall. But that's all Moonracer is – a picture and a dream! Galahad's a real live horse, with a personality all his own and feelings too, but you treat him as if he was a – a thing, like a robot, or some kind of oversized windup toy. You ride him once a day and then stick him in the barn all by himself the rest of the time, and that's just not right. Horses are sociable, sensitive animals. They need friends and companionship, but until Galahad met Speckles today he didn't have a friend in the world, not even you!"

Although Cam was still stunned she finally found her voice. "I can't believe you said that!" she cried. "I rescued him from Mr. Barnett, didn't I? I spent every cent I had and over a thousand dollars I *don't* have to get him healthy again. I feed him, and clean out his stall, and groom him. I take excellent care of Galahad – Doc told me so himself. If that's not being a friend, I'd like to know what is! What could I possibly do for him that I haven't already done?"

"You could try loving him a little," Lacey said softly.

78

"Love him? I don't even like him!" Cam scowled down at Galahad who was muzzling Speckles's neck. "He's stubborn, and sneaky, and bad-tempered. What's more, he doesn't like me, either."

"Why should he?" Lacey retorted. "Oh, sure you take good care of him. But you're not nice to him at all. You never speak kindly to him – I've never even seen you pat him. You expect him to go when you say go, and stop when you say stop. You yell at him when he does something wrong, but you never praise him or give him a reward when he does something right. No wonder Galahad acts the way he does! I bet you'd be mean and nasty too if your family treated you the way you treat him!"

Lacey broke off and bit her lip. "I'm really sorry, Cam," she said with a sigh. "I guess I shouldn't have shot off my big mouth like that, but I couldn't help it. I just can't stand seeing you and Galahad making each other miserable when you could be having so much fun, the way I do with Speckles. I guess you're pretty mad at me, huh?"

Cam hung her head. "No. I was, but I'm not anymore."

It was true. Her anger had slowly drained away as she listened to her friend. It had never occurred to Cam before that she might be to blame for Galahad's bad behavior, and now all she felt was guilt and shame. She knew that Lacey was absolutely right. She had treated him disgracefully.

Running her fingers through the gelding's reddish-brown mane, Cam thought back over the weeks since she had first seen him standing in the middle of the Montauk Highway. From that day to this Cam had regarded Galahad only as her ticket to the Centaurs. She cared *for* him, but she had never cared *about* him. True, Mr. Barnett had neglected and abused the horse, but then

79

so had Cam in a different, less obvious way. Galahad deserved better than that.

Feeling a little lower than slug slime, Cam forced a weak smile. "Okay, Dr. Vining. Now that you've diagnosed the problem, how about a cure?"

Laughing, Lacey said, "Take two aspirin and call me in the morning. You'll be getting my bill in the mail."

Cam shuddered. "Please! Don't mention bills!" Very seriously she said. "Tell me the truth, Lacey. Do you think it's too late to make it up to Galahad, or have I ruined him for good?"

"It's never too late," Lacey said as she untied Speckles from the fence.

"You're not leaving already, are you?" Cam asked anxiously.

"Yes, and so are you." Lacey led the mare over to the gate and opened it.

"Where are we going?"

"Anywhere, just as long as it's out of this pasture." Lacey replied, swinging into the saddle. "Riding around in a circle day after day would drive Speckles nuts, and I wouldn't be surprised if that's part of Galahad's problem, too."

Galahad was heading eagerly for the open gate, but Cam held him back. "Lacey, I really don't think he's ready –"

"Maybe you don't, but he does," she interrupted. "Let him do what he wants for a change. If he misbehaves, no big deal. We can always come back and try again tomorrow."

But Galahad didn't misbehave. In fact, Cam could hardly believe how docile and responsive he was. She was much too tense to enjoy herself when they first started out, afraid that at any moment the gelding would be up to his old tricks, but as he and Speckles walked nose to tail along the narrow dirt lane that bordered the cornfield, she gradually began to relax. Cam wasn't sure if it was leaving the pasture, having another horse for company, or a combination of both that made the difference in Galahad's attitude, and she didn't care. For whatever reason, he was acting like a perfect gentleman for the very first time.

When they emerged from the lane onto Skunk Hollow Road, Lacey suggested, "Let's head for the ocean and go for a canter on the beach. It'll be good practice for next Saturday. Besides, we always said we'd do that together someday, remember?"

"How could I forget? I even used to dream about riding Moonracer in the surf ..."

"Well, you're not dreaming now. You're wide awake," Lacey said briskly, turning Speckles toward the distant dunes. "This guy's name is Galahad, not Moonracer. And don't you dare say he's not ready!"

Cam shrugged, "Ready or not, here we come."

When Speckles started to trot, Galahad didn't need any urging to keep up. Cam gritted her teeth, prepared to endure the gelding's weird, jolting gait, but it seemed to have smoothed out miraculously. To her amazement, she discovered that she could actually post with no trouble at all. Galahad didn't shake his head or try to get the bit between his teeth, and he never once tried to snatch a mouthful of the wildflowers and weeds that grew temptingly close to the road.

"Good boy, Galahad," Cam murmured, patting his shoulder. "I'm really proud of you."

Lacey glanced over at her and smiled. "That's more like it!" she said.

Cam and Lacey had almost reached the dunes now. As

a fresh, salt-scented ocean breeze cooled Cam's burning cheeks, she suddenly realized that she was having a wonderful time. It had been so long since she had ridden purely for pleasure, she had almost forgotten how it felt.

The paved surface of the road stopped abruptly, replaced by a rutted track that led between the dunes then disappeared altogether into a broad expanse of smooth white sand. Beyond the beach the ocean, calm and flat today, stretched as far as Cam's eyes could see, sparkling like a million sapphires in the early-morning sunshine. It was still so early that there was nobody else in sight. Aside from the girls and their horses, the only other living things were a few gulls soaring high overhead. Cam and Lacey rode across the deserted beach to the water's edge. Neither Galahad nor Speckles had ever been so close to the ocean before, and they weren't sure they liked it. The girls gave them a few minutes to get used to the gentle ripples lapping at their hooves before they started walking eastward along the hard-packed sand.

Turning to Lacey, Cam said, "This is too good to be true! Are you sure I'm not dreaming?"

"If you are, then I am too. Pretty neat, isn't it?" With a smug grin, Lacey added, "I hate to say I told you so, but …"

"But you told me so," Cam finished for her. "I'm really glad you did. And by the way," she said sheepishly, "thanks for showing me what a pigheaded, selfish, obnoxious jerk I've been."

Lacey giggled. "Hey, what are friends for?" She gave Speckles a nudge with her heels, and as the mare broke into a canter, she called over her shoulder, "Come on, slowpokes! Catch us if you can!"

SEVEN

AFTER A GLORIOUS GALLOP ON THE BEACH, Lacey and Cam rode back to the farm. Promising to return the next day, Lacey headed for Seabreeze Stables. Galahad and Speckles whinnied to each other until the mare was out of sight.

"I know – you miss your friend already. But don't worry, fellow. She'll be back tomorrow," Cam told the dejected gelding as she started to lead him into the barn. "I can't believe how stupid I was not to know how lonely you were …"

"Cam, where've you been?"

At the sound of Ruthie's shrill voice, Cam turned around and saw her little sister hurrying toward her. "I went for a ride with Lacey," she said. "Why? Is something wrong?"

"Not anymore. I mean, I thought there was but now it's okay." Seeing Cam's puzzled expression, Ruthie said all in one breath, "I know you don't like anybody hanging around when you give Galahad his lesson but I sneaked over to the pasture anyway because I wanted to watch and you weren't there and the gate was open so I thought maybe he ran away with you and threw you into a ditch somewhere!"

Laughing, Cam said, "Nothing even remotely like that

happened. We had a great ride. In fact, Galahad behaved himself so well that I want to give him a reward. You don't have any carrots on you, by any chance?"

Ruthie stared at her. "No. Anyway, I thought you said they weren't good for him."

"I did, but I was wrong," Cam admitted. "It seems I've been wrong a lot lately. Listen, Ruthie, while I take off Galahad's tack, why don't you go pull some carrots? When you come back, we can give them to him, and then you can help me cool him down and groom him. You'll have to learn your way around a horse before you ride Galahad, and that's as good a way as any to begin."

Ruthie's face lit up like a Christmas tree. "Oh, wow!" she gasped. "Are you really going to teach me to ride him?"

"Sure. Not right away, though. I'll need to train him some more until he's completely comfortable with someone on his back. We won't be working out in the pasture very much anymore, but when we do, you can watch us if you like. You don't have to sneak around."

Her sister peered at her. "Are you sure Galahad didn't dump you on your head? You're acting awfully weird!"

"What do you mean, weird?" Cam asked.

"Nice," Ruthie replied promptly. "Like you used to be before you got Galahad."

For the second time that morning, Cam felt heartily ashamed of herself. "Oh, Ruthie," she sighed, "I'm so sorry! I know I've been a real pain, but from now on I'll be better, I promise."

Galahad had been standing patiently while the sisters talked, but his patience had come to an end. He pawed the ground and butted Cam in the back with his head.

"Okay, okay! You made your point," she said with a laugh.

Ruthie grinned. "I think he wants his carrots. I guess I'd better get them for him. Big ones or little ones?" she asked Cam.

"Big ones," Cam said. "He's earned them!"

That day marked the beginning of a whole new relationship between Cam and Galahad. Cam was determined to make up for how badly she'd treated him, so instead of forcing him to obey she concentrated on winning Galahad's trust. Her efforts paid off more rapidly than she could ever have imagined. The change in Galahad's attitude was so remarkable that he seemed like a different horse, and day by day her affection for him grew. Now that she had stopped thinking of him as a third-rate substitute for the impossibly perfect Moonracer, Cam was finally able to appreciate the gelding for the unique, often quirky, individual he was.

Cam and Lacey rode together again on Sunday, and as often during the next week as Lacey's schedule at the hardware store would permit. Although Galahad always behaved beautifully with Speckles, Cam had worried that he would be hard to handle once they were on their own. If she still had trouble controlling him by Saturday, she knew her parents wouldn't allow her to go to the Centaurs' cookout.

But to her delight Galahad's mellow mood didn't disappear with Speckles, and each day when they returned to the barn after their early-morning workout Cam lavished the gelding with praise and rewarded him with a treat. In fact, she never came to his stall or led him out to the pasture without bringing him an apple or couple of carrots. It didn't take Galahad long to realize that he had a good thing going, and the minute she entered the barn he would stick his head out over the door, nickering a greedy greeting.

Sometimes after Ruthie helped Cam groom her horse, the girls played a game with him that Ruthie made up. They hid a treat in one of their pockets or held it behind their backs and let Galahad search for it. His warm breath tickled, making Cam and Ruthie giggle as he sniffed and nuzzled them all over until he found his prize.

Cam also encouraged her older brothers and sisters to visit him as often as they liked and to bring him goodies. "Anything but sugar," she told them. "It really isn't good for his teeth."

Nathan and Natalie took her at her word and experimented with offering Galahad samples of their least favorite vegetables. "I don't believe this guy! He's a four-legged garbage can!" Nathan said on Thursday as Galahad gobbled up some broccoli, cauliflower, and zucchini, then peered around hopefully for more.

"He is not," Cam protested, stroking the gelding's neck. "Don't talk about my horse like that. You'll hurt his feelings."

Natalie shot her a skeptical glance. "Come on, Cam! You don't really think horses understand what people say, do you?"

"Maybe not every single word, but I'm sure this horse knows when somebody's making fun of him," she said huffily. "Galahad's pretty sensitive. He's intelligent, too."

"Boy, you sure have changed your tune," Nathan said. "You never used to have anything good to say about him, and now all of a sudden you're his one-girl cheering section. How come?"

Cam smiled. "I guess you could say I've been dreaming, but I got a wake-up call just in the nick of time."

The twins had no idea what she was talking about. They looked at each other, raised their eyebrows, and shrugged.

Nathan patted Galahad's nose. "Arugula tomorrow, fella," he promised.

When Nathan and Natalie left, Cam put her arms around the gelding's neck and gave him a hug. "Don't mind them," she said. "They just don't realize how special you are. I guess that's not so surprising, though – I only found out myself a little while ago. You're the best horse in the world, Galahad, and I love you a whole lot. Can you forgive me for being so hard on you before?"

Nodding his head, Galahad whuffled softly. Cam laughed. "And Nat doesn't think you understand what people say!"

Early Friday morning Cam invited her mother and father to watch her ride Galahad around the pasture. She wanted them to have no doubt in their minds about her ability to handle him on the next evening's trail ride. When she had put the gelding through his paces with ease, she trotted him over to the fence. "Well, what do you think?" she asked, patting Galahad proudly. "Isn't he terrific?"

"You're both terrific, Cam," Mr. Porter said. "I wouldn't have believed it if I hadn't seen it with my own two eyes. It's amazing what a lot of hard work and a little TLC can do."

"You've done a wonderful job with him," Mrs. Porter agreed. "I have to admit your father and I have been afraid that Operation Galahad would turn into Mission Impossible, but you proved us wrong. Congratulations, sweetheart!"

"It wasn't all me," Cam said quickly, "not by a long shot. I was going about it all wrong. If it wasn't for Lacey and Speckles, Galahad would probably still be fighting me tooth and nail." She grinned. "Make that tooth and *hoof*! So it's okay about the trail ride tonight? You'll let me go?"

Her father nodded, and her mother said, "I've got two

87

apple-crumb pies in the oven at this very minute. And speaking of which ..." She took a bright red apple out of her pocket. "Can I give this to him?"

Galahad eyed the apple and bobbed his head up and down, giving an eager little snort.

"Well now, I don't know about that, Ruth-Ann," Mr. Porter said solemnly. "I've heard that the horse is the only animal that eats better without a bit in its mouth."

Cam giggled. "Oh, Daddy, that's so corny! Go ahead, Mom. I don't care if it messes up Galahad's bit."

After the gelding devoured the apple in one big bite, Mr. Porter went off to load the pickup with produce for the farm stand, and Mrs. Porter returned to the kitchen to keep an eye on her baking.

"It's really going to happen, Galahad," Cam said to her horse. "We're going to be riding with the Centaurs tonight, and you'll make lots of new friends. And I wouldn't be surprised if I did, too!"

The members of the riding club were to gather at Seabreeze Stables at six o'clock, but there were so many customers at the roadside stand that Cam didn't get back to the farmhouse until five-fifteen. She dashed to her room and exchanged her shorts and sneakers for jeans and boots. Then, after grabbing her riding helmet and tying a sweater around her waist in case it got chilly later on, she raced to the barn to give Galahad a quick polishing.

"I know I groomed you after our morning ride, but I want you to look your absolute best for our first outing with the Centaurs," Cam told him as she combed his mane and tail and rubbed him all over with a soft cloth.

When she was satisfied that his chestnut coat was as

glossy as she could possibly make it, she tacked Galahad up and mounted. They started out for the boarding stable at a brisk jog trot.

While she rode, Cam ran over in her mind what Lacey had told her about the girls in the club. Aside from Lacey herself, Marjorie Ralston, Carla Luchese, and Diane Steinberg were the only ones Cam knew, because they all went to the same school. Like Lacey, they were "townies" who lived in Shorehaven and boarded their horses at Seabreeze. The others, Erica Hudson, Brenda Grimes, Tamara Benning, and Megan Ricker, lived in Brightwater, the next village to the west, and went to South Fork High. Cam wasn't sure where they kept their mounts.

Now let's see if I've got this straight, she thought. *Carla's club treasurer and her horse is a bay gelding named Gremlin. Diane's vice president. She has a bay, too, but it's a mare and her name is Lightfoot. Megan is president. She has a gray gelding called Stormy, and Erica's sorrel is Hotshot – or is Hotshot Marjorie's pinto? No, that's not right. Marjorie has a black mare, and her name is Brenda ... Wait a minute! Brenda's not a horse, she's club secretary! Okay, I'd better start all over. Diane's pinto gelding is named Stormy ...*

By the time Cam and Galahad reached Seabreeze, Cam was hopelessly confused. It didn't help to find everybody mounted and waiting for her in the stable yard. In their helmets they all looked so much alike that Cam had difficulty even recognizing the girls from her own school – except Lacey, of course.

She trotted Speckles right over to Cam and Galahad, grinning from ear to ear. As the two horses greeted each other with their usual happy snuffles and snorts, Lacey cried,

"Hail, fellow Centaur! You made it! We were beginning to wonder if you'd changed your mind."

Cam grinned, too. "No way! Sorry I'm late, but I got tied up at the stand."

"Well, you're here now, and that's what counts." Turning Speckles to face the other riders, Lacey said, "For those of you who don't know her, this is Cam Porter, the friend I told you about, and her horse Galahad."

Everybody smiled, and a round-faced, slightly heavyset girl wearing glasses and riding a handsome gray came forward. "Pleased to meet you, Cam. I'm Megan, and this fellow here ..." she patted the gray's shoulder, "... is Stormy. In my official capacity as club president, I take great pleasure in welcoming you to the South Shore Centaurs."

Several of the girls snickered, and Carla said, "Come off it, Megan! Cam's going to think we're a bunch of stuffed shirts!"

Megan laughed. "Hey, give me a break. How often do I have a chance to be really pompous? Just let me tell our new member who's who and then we'll hit the road."

She quickly introduced Cam to Brenda and her bay gelding Pretty Boy, Tamara and her pinto Pirate, and Erica and her sorrel Hotshot.

At least I got one of them right! Cam thought. Aloud, she said to Megan, "I already know the Shorehaven crowd – or at least I know who they are."

"Great! In that case, let's get a move on. We want to get to the beach in time to catch the sunset over the ocean. It ought to be a fantastic one tonight."

Megan and Stormy led the way out of the stable yard and turned down a lane shaded by tall, graceful elms. Cam and Lacey brought up the rear, and Carla fell back to join them on Gremlin, her bay gelding.

Eyeing Galahad as he stepped along with ears pricked forward and neck arched, she said, "Nice horse. I like the way he holds his head."

"He's having the time of his life," Cam said. "Until tonight, I think Galahad believed he and Speckles were the only horses in the world!"

"But don't be jealous, girl. You'll always be his very best friend," Lacey assured the mare.

"I thought you said Cam bought a broken-down old beast from some farmer," Carla said to Lacey. "Plug-Ugly, you said his name was. Whatever happened to him?"

"Plenty!" Cam glanced at Lacey, and they both cracked up.

"Cam's fairy godmother came along and waved her magic wand." Lacey giggled.

"Yeah, and poof! The ugly duckling turned into a swan!"

"The frog turned into a prince!"

"Beauty turned into the Beast – oops, I mean the other way around!"

By now Cam and Lacey were laughing so hard that the riders in front of them turned around to stare. Carla stared at them, too. "What's with you two? All I asked was what happened to Cam's other horse. I don't see what's so funny about that."

"I'm sorry," Cam gasped between giggles. "It's just that there is no other horse! This is him!"

More puzzled than ever, Carla asked, "Who's him?"

Cam pointed at Galahad.

Carla's jaw dropped. "He's him?" Lacey and Cam nodded. "Get out of here! From the way Lacey described that horse, he sounded like a reject from the glue factory! Are you sure you guys aren't putting me on?"

"Cross my heart and hope to die," Lacey said solemnly.

"I wanted to keep it a secret until everybody saw him, but Plug-Ugly and Sir Galahad here are one and the same. Only, there wasn't any fairy godmother. Cam transformed him all by herself."

"Really? That's incredible!" Carla exclaimed.

"No wonder, because it's not true," Cam said, smiling at Lacey.

"Oh, okay. Speckles and I helped a little ..."

"A lot! And so did the vet, and the blacksmith, and my family. But it only worked because we had good material to start with." Cam patted Galahad's shoulder proudly. "He's one extra-special horse."

Lacey made a face at her. "It's about time you figured that out!"

"That is so neat," Carla said. "Wait till I tell the others!" She trotted Gremlin up to Brenda and Tamara, and Cam could hear her begin. "You're not going to believe this, but you know that total wreck of a horse Lacey told us about, the one Cam bought for two cents? Well ..."

"Galahad, old buddy, you're about to be famous," Lacey said to the gelding. "Try not to let it go to your head!"

The news of Cam's "Cinderella horse" quickly spread down the line, and Galahad was all anybody talked about for the next few minutes. Several of the girls rode back to check him out at closer range and to compliment Cam on what an amazing job she'd done.

They soon left the country lane with its overhanging trees, however, and picked up a much narrower trail, which meant the Centaurs had to ride single file. That was fine with Cam. Although she had been pleased by the attention Galahad was receiving, she was perfectly content just to amble along on her horse, appreciating the peaceful beauty of the evening.

The sun was very low in the western sky, and its slanting golden rays lit the backs of the horses and riders, casting long purple shadows before them. The trail wound through a landscape that gradually changed from meadowlands to salt marshes where mallow roses and sea lavender flourished among the whispering reeds, and finally to the dune covered with beach grass waving like a green and silver sea in the ocean breeze.

The beach to which the Centaurs were heading was far enough away from the clusters of cottages crowding much of the shore that very few bathers ever made the trek from the public-use areas. When they reached it, the only other people in sight were two men and a woman. Cam recognized Mr. Vining, but she didn't know who the other two people were. They were taking things out of several huge coolers and putting them on a folding table that had been set up on the sand. A driftwood fire was already crackling merrily nearby.

Lacey waved and her father waved back. "Dad and Erica's parents were drafted to bring the food and act as chaperones tonight," she called to Cam over the pounding of the surf. "Did you remember about the pie?"

Cam nodded. "*Two* pies – apple-crumb."

"All right! My favorite!"

They followed the other riders a little way down the beach to a place at the base of the dune where several weathered timbers stuck out of the sand.

"Mosey on up to the hitchin' post, podners," Marjorie drawled in a fake Western accent as she tied Dawn, her black mare, to one of the pieces of wood.

Lacey and Cam dismounted and tethered their horses as well. After they had given Speckles and Galahad the carrots

93

they'd brought with them, Lacey, Marjorie, and the others headed back to the cookout site, but Cam lingered.

"Pretty neat, isn't it?" she said to Galahad, stroking his warm, silky neck. "We'll be doing lots of things like this even though summer's just about over." The horse swung his head from side to side and snorted. Laughing, Cam said, "Yeah, I know how you feel. I can hardly believe school will be starting next week. But I'll spend as much time with you as I can. We'll ride with Lacey and Speckles after school and with the Centaurs on weekends. And then there's the Santa Claus Parade in November ..."

"Hey, Cam, hurry up!" One of the girls shouted. "You're missing one of the greatest sunsets of all time!"

Cam gave Galahad one last pat and ran off to join her friends.

EIGHT

ALTHOUGH CAM HAD PUSHED THE THOUGHT
of Dr. Connors' bill to the back of her mind, she hadn't
forgotten about it. She had been hoarding every cent of her
allowance, and now that September was here, Cam told
herself each day as she got ready for school that she would
call the clinic and work out a payment plan with Doc's
receptionist. But she just couldn't bring herself to do it,
afraid that Mrs. Grayson would insist on larger installments
than she was able to afford. Day after day slipped by, and
by the third week in September Cam still hadn't called.

She had managed to avoid telling her mother and father
how much she owed, saying only that Doc was allowing
her to pay it off over a period of time. Cam's parents had
enough problems without worrying about her debt. Mr.
and Mrs. Porter never burdened their children with their
financial troubles, but Cam knew they were having a harder
time than usual making ends meet.

Bonnie's tuition at Halsey College had gone up, and due
to the unusually rainy spring and early summer profits from
the farm were down. There were no new back-to-school
clothes for Cam or her brothers and sisters. In late August,
Bonnie had taken a part-time job at an art-supply store in

Southampton to pay some of her college expenses. Natalie baby-sat as often as she could, and at the beginning of September Scott had gotten Nathan an after-school job at the gas station where he worked several nights a week. The only ones who still received an allowance were Cam and Ruthie.

"Even though my folks say it's really a salary because I earn it, I hate taking money from them," Cam said to Lacey as they ate lunch in the cafeteria with Carla, Marjorie, and Diane. Cam had brought a tuna sandwich from home because she didn't want to spend a cent unless it was absolutely necessary. "I mean, it's okay for Ruthie. She's just a little kid with no responsibilities, but I've got Galahad and he's costing a lot more than I thought he would. Do you think your father might give me a part-time job at the hardware store?"

Lacey looked up from her pasta salad and shook her head. "Sorry, Cam. He's not hiring anybody. Business was really lousy this summer, and it's even worse now that the tourist season's over. Dad's only keeping me on because I'm his daughter and I work dirt cheap."

"Things are tough all over." Diane sighed. "I had a great summer job at Connie's Cookies, but they laid me off at the end of July. I was kicking in most of my salary to help cover Lightfoot's board. Now my parents have to pay the whole thing, and you should hear them gripe about it."

"Mine do, too. And I just heard a rumor that Seabreeze is going to raise their rates," Marjorie said around a mouthful of chili.

Carla almost choked on her cheeseburger. "You've gotta be kidding! They're sky-high now! If that happens, I'll have to stable Gremlin in our garage."

"Is it a two-car garage? Because if it is, Gremlin's going to have a roommate," Diane joked.

96

"You're not so bad off, Cam," Marjorie said. "At least you don't have to pay boarding fees for Galahad."

"Yeah, but I have to feed him and pay his vet bill. You wouldn't believe how much Doc Connors charged for getting him back in shape. Galahad's worth every penny, of course," Cam added loyally, "but it's still an awful lot of money."

"Have you talked to Doc's receptionist about how you're going to pay it off?" Lacey asked.

Cam shook her head. "Not yet. I've been putting it off, but I'm definitely going to call the clinic when I get home today."

Carla giggled. "Good luck!"

Cam didn't like the sound of that. "What are you talking about?" she asked nervously. "Is she nasty?"

"Oh, no," Carla assured her with a grin. "Mrs. Grayson's a real nice old lady, but she's flakier than the Pillsbury Doughboy!"

Later that afternoon when Cam phoned the vet clinic from her parents' room, she discovered what Carla meant.

"Shorehaven Veterinary Clinic. May I help you?" chirped a woman's voice.

"Mrs. Grayson? This is Cambria Porter. My horse is a patient of Dr. Connors, and –"

"Oh, my, that's too bad, dear," Mrs. Grayson interrupted. "What's wrong with the poor animal? The doctor is in surgery right now, so unless it's an emergency, I'll give him the message as soon as he's free and he'll call you back. Or you could talk to Dr. Marx. I'm sure he's here somewhere."

"It's not an emergency. Galahad's perfectly fine, but –"

"If nothing's wrong with him, why do you want to speak to the doctor?" the woman snapped. "He's a very busy man, you know."

97

"I *don't* want to speak to him. Doc treated my horse a while back, and when he gave me his bill, he told me to speak to *you* about setting up a payment plan," Cam explained patiently.

"Well, why didn't you say so in the first place? What's the name again? Potter?"

"Porter. With an *r*."

"All right. Now let me see if I can find your file on this darned computer ..."

There was a long silence.

"Mrs. Grayson, are you still there?" Cam asked at last.

"Yes, yes, here I am. We just got this machine last week and I'm still not quite sure how it works. Uh-oh – wrong button ... Oh, dear, now what have I done? I'll never understand why we can't keep real files in folders the way we used to in the old days. It was so much simpler that way ..." After another long pause, Mrs. Grayson exclaimed triumphantly, "Aha! Here it is! Sailor Porter. Thirty-five dollars for a checkup and booster shots."

"I'm afraid not, Mrs. Grayson," Cam said. "Sailor's our dog. I'm pretty sure my dad paid that bill last month. I'm talking about my *horse*, Galahad."

"Gallagher?"

"*Galahad*," Cam shouted into the received. "Like the knight of King Arthur's Round Table."

"Hmmmm ... I don't see him here under Porter. Just a minute. Maybe I filed him under G ... no, not there either. Could I have filed him under H for horse? Oh, dear! I can't seem to find him anywhere, and there's a call on the other line. I'm going to try to put on you hold, Catherine. Be right back. Now which button am I supposed to push ...?"

Before Cam could tell the woman that her name was

Cambria, not Catherine, the dial tone buzzed in her ear. Cam hung up, waited a moment, and then dialed the clinic's number again. This time she got a busy signal. On the third try, a youngish male voice answered.

"Could I please speak to Mrs. Grayson?" Cam said. "I was talking to her a few minutes ago, but then she put me on hold and lost me."

The guy sighed. "That happens a lot. Sorry, but she just left for the day – dentist appointment. Maybe I can help you."

Cam thought he sounded like a fairly sensible person, so she told him her story – or started to. "Well, Dr. Connors took care of my horse a while back, and when he gave me his bill, he told me to talk to Mrs. Grayson about paying it off on the installment plan, so ..."

"Gee, I wouldn't know anything about that," he said. "I'm only Doc's assistant, covering the phones while Mrs. G's gone. Billing's her department. You better call back tomorrow."

"Okay," Cam said with a helpless shrug. So much for trying to get the bill straightened out. "Thanks anyway."

"No problem. Have a nice day."

Cam replaced the receiver, then hurried downstairs to the kitchen to help her mother make spaghetti sauce with the last of the tomatoes. With any luck, when they were finished she'd still have time to take Galahad for a nice long ride before supper.

The following afternoon, Cam steeled herself to call the clinic again. When Mrs. Grayson answered the phone, she didn't sound nearly as chirpy as she had the day before.

"Oh, yes, Carolyn," she mumbled after Cam had identified herself. "I'm terribly sorry I had to leave in such a rush yesterday, but I've been having dreadful trouble with my teeth. Dr. Fishbein pulled two molars, and let me tell you, it hurt like the dickens! I've taken so many pain pills that I'm positively groggy."

"Gee, that's too bad, Mrs. Grayson," Cam said politely. "About the bill for my horse, Galahad ..."

"Yes, of course. Where were we? Oh, now I remember – I couldn't find him on that computer machine, so I asked Dr. Connors about it this morning and he explained your situation. What sort of payment schedule did you have in mind, dear?"

Cam had thought about this a lot, and now she said, "I could probably manage twenty-five dollars –"

"That will be fine," Mrs. Grayson said. "I'll make a note of it. Twenty-five dollars a week."

"Uh … I'm afraid not," Cam swallowed hard. "Not a week. A *month*."

Mrs. Grayson gasped. "Oh, no!" she moaned.

"I know it's not very much, but it's all I can afford," Cam confessed miserably.

"I simply can't believe this," the woman muttered. "I'll have to talk to the doctor immediately!"

Cam was speechless with dismay. Although she knew the amount she had mentioned was pitifully small, she certainly hadn't expected such an extreme reaction. One awful possibility after another raced through her mind. What if Dr. Connors demanded that she pay more? Could he take Galahad away and hold him hostage while she whittled away at her debt? What if the vet went to her parents? What if ...?

Before Cam could beg for mercy, Mrs. Grayson wailed, "My poor mouth! It's bleeding all over my brand-new silk blouse!"

It took a second for Cam to realize that Mrs. Grayson was upset about her dental problems, not about what Cam had said. When she did, she went limp with relief. "Then twenty-five dollars a month is okay?" she asked eagerly.

"Yes, yes, fine. I'm sorry to do this to you again, Catherine, but I've got to call Dr. Fishbein before I bleed to death!"

Feeling guilty because she was so happy when Mrs. Grayson was so distressed, Cam was about to offer her sympathy, but Mrs. Grayson had already hung up.

Cam decided she would make her first payment on Saturday. After the Centaurs' meeting on Friday night, she was sleeping over at Lacey's house. In the morning Cam and Lacey could take the bus to the vet clinic, where Cam would hand over the cash in person.

She told Lacey about her plan while they rode their horses together later that afternoon. "And then I'll only have nine hundred seventy-five dollars to go," she finished.

"Only!" Lacey rolled her eyes. "That's still an awful lot, Cam."

"I know. But as soon as I can start earning money on my own, I'll be able to pay more," Cam said. "I figure I'll be out from under in – oh, about three years max, maybe two if I'm lucky."

"And if nothing goes wrong."

"Nothing will," Cam stated. "I won't let it!"

On Friday evening, Bonnie dropped Cam off at Lacey's house right after supper so they could get ready for the meeting of the South Shore Centaurs. They popped enough popcorn for an army, and set out big bottles of soda and plenty of paper cups in the Vinings' family room.

101

The meeting was scheduled for seven thirty, but Carla, Marjorie, and Diane arrived around seven. The girls from Brightwater all came a little later in Megan's car. She was the oldest member of the club and had just gotten her driver's license.

When the cat-shaped clock on the wall above the stone fireplace wagged its tail and meowed three times signaling the half hour, Megan hauled herself up from the plaid couch where she had been scarfing down popcorn and soda and announced, "This meeting will now come to order, I guess. The first order of business is the reading of the minutes from the last meeting."

Tamara waved a hand. "Madam President, I move that we bag the minutes. Who cares about them anyway?"

"Good idea," Megan agreed. "Second, anybody?"

"I second the motion," Marjorie said through a mouthful of popcorn.

"Me, too," Carla called out.

Marjorie poked her in the ribs. "You can't do that. I already seconded it."

"Okay, then I third it!"

"I fourth it," Lacey yelled.

"The motion has been seconded, thirded, and fourthed," Megan said with a straight face. "All in favor say aye."

"Aye-yi-yi!" everybody else, including Cam, shouted. Since this was her first Centaurs meeting, she had been a little nervous, not knowing what to expect. Now that she saw it was all in fun, she felt much more comfortable.

"So much for the minutes," Megan said. "Marjorie brought a video of the jumping competition at the last Olympics that I know we all want to see, so what say we skip old business and get right on to new, exciting business?

I've got some great news! The Shorehaven Chamber of Commerce wants the Centaurs to participate in the Santa Claus Parade this November."

Eric yawned. "What's the big deal? We were in the parade last year, too."

"The big deal," Megan replied, "is that they don't want us to just ride in the parade. They want us to lead the Santa Claus float!"

Erica woke up right away. "Now that's more like it," she cried.

"Wow!" "Cool!" "Terrific!" several girls exclaimed all at the same time.

"Last year they stuck us between the Historical Society float and the bagpipe band," Brenda said to Cam and Lacey. "It was the worst position in the whole parade."

"Tell me about it," Tamara groaned. "The truck the float was on spewed out so much exhaust that we nearly suffocated, and the bagpipes drove the horses crazy!"

"Well, we won't have any of those problems this time," Diane said. "The Santa Claus float is always the very last one in the parade, and we'll probably be following a bunch of Brownie troops or Cub Scouts."

"The Brownies looked so cute last year, all wrapped up like Christmas packages," Marjorie said.

"Uh-uh. The Christmas packages were the kids in that dance class, not the Brownies," Tamara corrected. "The Brownies were snowmen, I think ..."

"Pipe down, everybody!" Megan hollered. When the chatter had died away, she went on. "Speaking of costumes, I forgot to mention that the Chamber of Commerce is offering a prize of fifty dollars to the group with the best costumes."

"Hey, neat!" Carla exclaimed. "If we win, we'll actually have some money for a change! It's not much fun being club treasurer when there's no treasury."

"Lacey and I saw you riding in the parade last year," Cam said. "You were all wearing red or green sweats and Santa hats. What were you supposed to be, anyway?"

"Beats me," Diane said with a shrug. "We just wanted to look Christmassy. But we'll have to come up with something really special this time if we want a crack at that prize."

"Our horses ought to have costumes, too," Lacey put in. "After all, they're the most important part of our group."

"We'd better start thinking about this right now. November will be here before we know it. Anybody have any ideas?" Megan asked.

The girls thought about it for a minute. Suddenly Erica's hand shot up. "I just had a terrific one! Listen to this – we all dress in white and wrap ourselves with silver tinsel, the kind you put on Christmas trees. Then we spray the horses with glue and sprinkle them with silver glitter and drape them with tinsel, too!"

"Sounds weird to me," Marjorie said doubtfully. "What would we be – angels?"

Erica scowled at her. "Angels? Get real! We'd be snowflakes!"

"Gee, Erica, that might be nice, but wouldn't it be awfully expensive to buy so much tinsel and glitter and glue?" Carla asked.

"Also, I don't have any white winter clothes, and I don't want to ask my folks to buy me a new outfit just for the parade," Diane said. "They're kind of strapped for cash these days."

"Mine, too. And even if we could afford it, which we

can't, there's no way I'm covering Pretty Boy with all that junk," Brenda stated firmly.

When the others agreed with her, Megan said, "Sorry, Erica. Thanks anyway. Let's hear some other suggestions."

Cam had been thinking hard, and now she raised her hand. "What about reindeer?"

"Reindeer?" Megan echoed.

"Yeah," Cam said eagerly. "Our horses could be Santa's reindeer! We could make antlers out of cardboard or something and attach them to the brow bands of their bridles. Maybe we could make wreaths with big red bows to put around their necks, too. I bet my sister Bonnie would help – she's good at stuff like that. She always makes our Christmas wreaths and last year she even made reindeer antlers for our dog."

Lacey thought that was a great idea. "The horses would be the reindeer, and we'd be Santa's elves. You guys could wear the same stuff you wore last year so nobody would have to buy anything new," she pointed out. "I'm sure Cam and I can dig up a couple of Santa hats, and I've got red sweats at home. I bet Nat has something you could borrow, right, Cam?"

Cam nodded. "It wouldn't cost anybody a cent!"

"Sounds good to me," Carla said.

"Me too. Super idea, Cam. What about the rest of you?" Megan asked. "All in favor, say aye."

There was a chorus of "ayes" from everybody, even a reluctant one from Erica, who was still pouting a little.

Megan smiled. "Okay, that's settled. Since we won't have to worry about making the antlers and wreaths until November, let's talk about Sunday's trail ride. We'll meet at Seabreeze as usual –"

"Hold it!" Brenda cut in. "I just thought of something. Santa's only got eight reindeer, and there are nine of us."

"You forgot about Rudolph 'with his nose so bright,'" Diane said. "One of our horses ought to be Rudolph. Whoever it is can go in front and the rest of us can ride behind two by two."

Tamara giggled. "Listen to this! My dad's an electrician, and I bet he could make a big red nose that lights up. Maybe he could even make it blink!"

"That would be so cool! With a light-up nose, we'd be sure to win the prize," Lacey said. "But which horse should be Rudolph?"

Naturally, each girl thought her horse should be chosen for such a major role in the Santa Claus Parade. Cam listened in silence to the discussion that followed. As the newest member of the club, she didn't want to seem pushy. She also didn't want to get involved in the argument, which was becoming more and more heated by the minute.

Cam was beginning to wish she had never come up with the reindeer idea when Megan said loudly, "Listen up, you guys! This is ridiculous. There's no point in calling for a vote, because we'll each vote for our own horse, so it seems to me the only fair way to decide is by drawing straws. Short straw wins."

"Nine straws coming up." Lacey sprang up from her seat on the couch next to Cam and went over to the hearth, where she took the little broom from the set of fireplace tools. She pulled out a handful of straws, counted out nine, then snapped off the end of one of them and mixed them all up. "Here you go, Madam Pres," she said, handing the straws to Megan with a flourish.

"This never would have happened if everybody'd gone

along with my snowflake theme," Erica grumbled as she pulled the first straw. "Rats! Long! Just my luck."

Marjorie, Brenda, Diane, and Lacey all drew long straws, too. Then it was Cam's turn. She grabbed one of the four remaining straws in Megan's fist and pulled it out. Even before Cam saw it herself, Lacey cried, "It's Galahad! You got the short one!"

Cam stared at the straw in astonishment, feeling both pleased and uneasy. "Maybe we ought to do this again," she mumbled. "I mean, it doesn't seem right that Galahad and I get to lead the club in the parade when we've only just joined."

Carla spoke up. "Don't be silly, Cam! You won fair and square. It's great that your horse is going to be Rudolph – right, gang?" she asked the others.

"Right!" Marjorie called out, and started to sing, "*Galahad* the red-nosed reindeer had a very shiny nose ..."

Laughing, the rest of the girls chimed in, "And if you ever saw it, you would even say it glows!"

A grin slowly spread over Cam's face. She couldn't help thinking that the role of Rudolph was perfect for Galahad. The other reindeer had laughed at Rudolph and called him names because he was different. People had made fun of Galahad and called him names, too, but they would never do that anymore. Cam's horse, the horse nobody wanted, was going to be a star of the Santa Claus Parade!

NINE

RUTHIE WAS EVERY BIT AS THRILLED AS CAM about Galahad's being chosen to lead the Centaurs in the parade. She was his second-biggest fan in the Porter family, and she spent almost as much time with the chestnut gelding as Cam did herself. Ruthie never stopped begging Cam to teach her to ride him, and by the second week in October Cam decided her horse had mellowed out enough for their lessons to begin.

Early one bright, crisp Saturday morning after Ruthie had helped her feed Galahad, change his bedding, groom him, and tack him up, Cam led him into the barnyard with her little sister dancing at her side. Ruthie was wearing Cam's helmet and a pair of boots Cam had outgrown, and her freckled face glowed with excitement.

Cam had adjusted the length of Galahad's stirrup leathers for Ruthie's short legs. Now she halted the horse by the fence so Ruthie could stand on one of the rails to mount him.

"Why do you always have to get on from the left side?" Ruthie asked.

Cam shrugged. "I don't know. You just do, that's all. Remember how I showed you to hold the reins?"

Ruthie nodded eagerly. "Sure. I've practiced dozens of times."

"Good. Now gather them up, put your foot in the stirrup, and climb aboard."

Ruthie did as she was told. When she plopped herself down on the saddle, Galahad looked mildly surprised.

"I know." Cam gave him a reassuring pat. "It's not me, but it's okay. I'll be right here every minute."

"I did it!" Ruthie said with a proud grin. Her grin wobbled a little, however when she glanced down at the ground. "Wow! Galahad sure is *high*!"

"Relax, Ruthie. You won't fall off," Cam said. "I'll be leading Galahad today, and all we'll do is walk. Ready?"

Ruthie nodded again. As Cam began to lead the gelding around the barnyard at a slow, measured pace, Ruthie said, "Horses are my most favorite animals in the whole world. You're so lucky, Cam! As soon as I'm old enough, I'm going to have a horse just like Galahad and join the Centaurs the way you did." She sighed. "That won't be for an awfully long time, though."

"Probably not," Cam agreed. "I've wanted my own horse ever since I was a lot younger than you are. If I hadn't found Galahad, I'd still be dreaming about Moonracer ..." All of a sudden she had an idea. "Say, Ruthie, how would you like to borrow him?"

Ruthie's eyes widened. "Galahad?"

Laughing, Cam said, "No, dopey! Moonracer. You can hang his picture on your wall if you want until the real thing comes along."

"You're kidding!" Ruthie squealed, making Galahad's ears flicker back and forth. "Can I really?"

"Why not? Moonracer's beautiful and I'll always love

him because he was my dream horse. But now that I've got Galahad, I don't need him anymore. I'm sure Scott and Bonnie will understand if I pass him along to you."

"Oh, thank you, Cam!" Ruthie breathed. "Now we're both lucky!"

Cam smiled. "You're right, Ruthie. We sure are."

The following Wednesday when she went to the barn to give Galahad his supper, Cam discovered to her dismay that she was almost out of feed. She had thought there was one more unopened sack, but she was wrong. Cam didn't know what to do. She had just made her second payment to the vet and was running very low on cash. Lacey offered to lend her some money, but Cam refused. She knew Lacey was turning over most of her salary from her job at the hardware store to her parents to help pay Speckles's board. Once again, Cam had to ask her father for help.

The next evening after supper she knocked on the half-open door of the room Mr. Porter used for his office and stuck her head inside.

"Daddy, can I talk to you for a minute?"

Her father was seated at his desk, buried in paperwork – probably bills, Cam thought guiltily. When he looked up at her, his smile was weary.

"Sure, honey," he said. "What's up?"

Cam came in and moved a stack of farming publications from the shabby armchair in front of the desk. Perching nervously on the edge of the chair, she said, "It's about Galahad, I made a mistake when I thought I had enough feed to last him through the end of the month," she confessed. "I need to buy more, but – well, I don't have the money right now. Do you think you could charge it to your account at the Agway? I'm really sorry, Daddy. You can keep this week's allowance to help pay for part of it, and next week's, too."

Her father hesitated a moment, then nodded slowly. "All right. I was planning on going into the village tomorrow anyway, so I'll pick you up after school. We can get the feed then."

"Thanks," Cam murmured, getting to her feet. "Maybe now that fall's here, Galahad won't eat so much. I think I read somewhere that horses eat less in cold weather – or is it more?"

"Let's hope it's less," Mr. Porter said dryly. "*Much* less. I've been going over my bills for the past couple of months, and what with the feed, the vitamins, and all of Galahad's other supplies, he's costing almost as much as the rest of the family put together."

He turned his attention back to his papers, and Cam tiptoed out of the office. If only she could find some way to help pay for Galahad's expenses! She went upstairs to do her homework, and as she passed Natalie's room, she had an idea.

Backtracking a few steps, she knocked on the door. "It's me, Cam. I have to talk to you."

"C'mon in," Natalie called.

Cam found her sister sprawled on the bed studying with two of the cats, Pluto and Saturn, curled up one on each side of her. Natalie muttered, "Whatever it is, make it quick, okay? I've got a beast of a test tomorrow morning."

Sitting on the bed, Cam said, "Listen, Nat, can I ask you a favor?"

Natalie frowned. "What kind of a favor?"

"Well, I really need some money, and ..."

"Forget it! I don't have an extra cent."

"That's not what I mean. I don't want to borrow from you," Cam said quickly. "I want a job."

"A job?" Natalie stared at her. "You want me to hire you? Are you out of your mind?"

"A baby-sitting job. It's the only way I can think of to earn money, but everybody we know with little kids uses you," Cam explained. "I was thinking I could fill in for you every now and then if you're too busy or something – like maybe on a Friday or Saturday night when you have a date?"

"Hmmm ..." After Natalie thought about it for a moment, her eyes lit up. "Mrs. Ferguson lined me up to baby-sit her kids this Saturday night way back before I started going steady with Jason. He asked me to go to the Harvest Dance at school, but I told him a couldn't because it's the same night. Want to take my place with the Ferguson brats?"

There was a Centaurs meeting that night at Brenda's house, but this was a lot more important, so Cam immediately decided to skip it. "Yes!" she cried.

"Great!" Natalie looked at her watch and leaped off the bed, startling the cats and scattering her earth science notes all over the floor. "It's still early – I'll call Jason to tell him we're on, and then I'll call Mrs. Ferguson. I'm sure it will be okay with her." She was halfway out the door when she turned back. "What do you need this money for, anyway?"

"For Galahad." Cam sighed. "His upkeep is costing a lot more than I thought it would."

"Maybe you ought to think about selling him," Natalie said. "That's what you said you were going to do when you first got him, and now that he's such a nice-looking horse, I bet you'd get a couple hundred dollars for him, or even more."

Cam bristled. "No way! Selling Galahad would be like – like selling a member of the family!"

"Hey, don't bite my head off, okay? It was just a suggestion. But you have to admit that a horse is kind of a luxury item, and with money as tight as it is around here lately ..." Natalie shrugged. "Well, it's none of my business. Guess I'd better make those calls."

A *luxury* item, Cam thought as she followed her sister out of the room. *If that's really what Galahad is, do I have a right to keep him?*

"I do if nobody else has to support him," she told herself. "And nobody else will. If I can just take over a few baby-sitting jobs, I'll be able to pay Daddy back pretty soon and maybe even give a little more to Doc Connors each month."

Then she remembered that Galahad was due for his autumn flu shot, adding yet another fee to the vet's bill. Would she never get out from under her burden of debt?

That night Cam dreamed she was riding Galahad on her parents' property, but it didn't look like the farm she knew and loved. The cornfields, orchards, and vegetable gardens had been replaced by a complex of condominiums that rose out of the bare earth. When she and Galahad approached the farmhouse, Cam was horrified to see her father nailing a big FOR SALE sign on its weathered gray shingles.

Looking down at her horse, she saw that his coat was covered with hundred-dollar bills, and she cried, "No, Daddy, wait! Don't sell the house! I've got plenty of money right here!" But when she tried to peel off some of the bills, they stuck to Galahad like glue.

The dream stuck with Cam the same way. Although she knew Galahad's bill at the Agway wouldn't really force her family to sell the farm, she was more determined than ever to pay her horse's way.

Early Saturday evening, Scott drove Cam to the Fergusons' farm. Nine-year-old Betsy Ferguson was a friend of Ruthie's, and her two little brothers were seven and four. In spite of what Natalie had said, they were well-behaved children, not bratty at all. Cam had no trouble keeping them amused until their bedtimes, and she was thrilled when Mr. Ferguson paid her what amounted to two weeks' allowance.

Mrs. Cantwell, one of Natalie's regular clients who lived in Shorehaven, called on Monday asking her to baby-sit on Thursday afternoon. Fortunately for Cam's pocketbook, Natalie had just made a date with Jason to go to a high-school football game after school that day, so Cam eagerly volunteered to take her sister's place looking after three-year-old Ian.

Unfortunately, although Ian looked like a curly-headed cherub, he turned out to be brattier than all three Ferguson children put together. The minute Cam walked through the door, he took one look at her and threw a fit. As Mrs. Cantwell tried to pry the howling child from her legs, she explained that Ian was a very sensitive little boy who was devoted to Natalie and didn't take kindly to any other baby-sitter.

"But I'm sure you'll have no trouble with him at all once he gets used to you," Mrs. Cantwell shouted over Ian's outraged screams as she edged out the door. "Just put his 'Sesame Street' videos on the VCR and he'll be quiet as a lamb until I come home."

It didn't quite work out that way, however. Ian whined,

whimpered, and wailed through three episodes of his favorite show. When Cam tried to read to him, he snatched the book from her hands and flung it across the room, and he poured the orange juice she gave him all over the dog. But it was worth it, because by the time Mr. Cantwell dropped her at her door at half past six, Cam was another ten dollars richer.

Thank goodness for Jason! She thought as she climbed the porch steps. *For Galahad's sake, I hope Natalie keeps dating him for a long, long time!*

Coming into the house, Cam sang out. "Hi, everybody! I'm home."

She dropped her backpack on the table by the door, hung her jacket in the hall closet, and stuck her head into the kitchen. "What's for supper, Mom? I'm starved!"

Mrs. Porter turned from the pot of stew she was stirring on the stove, and her expression was so serious that Cam's smile faded instantly. "Your father wants to speak to you right away, Cam," she said.

Cam's first thought was that something had happened to Galahad. She had let him out into the pasture before she left for school that morning, and she was absolutely sure she'd latched the gate securely. But what if she was wrong? What if her horse had gotten out again and run away? What if he'd tried to cross the highway and been hit by a car?

"Is it Galahad?" she asked anxiously. "He hasn't been hurt or anything, has he?"

"No, Galahad's fine. Ruthie took him back to his stall a little while ago. It was getting so chilly that she was afraid he'd catch cold."

"Oh, good!" Cam heaved a sigh of relief. "So what does Daddy want to talk to me about?"

115

"Galahad," Mrs. Porter said.

"But, Mom, you just said ..."

"There's nothing wrong with your horse, Cam. Heaven knows there shouldn't be, considering the size of Dr. Connors's bill!"

Cam felt as if her heart had just dropped down into her shoes. "D-Doc's b-bill?" she stammered. "How did you ...?"

"It came in the mail today. Please don't keep your father waiting. He's in his office."

Cam walked slowly down the hall on leaden feet. The office door was open, and her father was sitting at his desk. Without speaking, he held out a piece of paper. Cam took it and stared at the words printed there. It was a bill from the Shorehaven Veterinary Clinic made out to Harold Porter, and as Cam read it, her jaw dropped.

"For veterinary services rendered – Galahad, chestnut gelding: $1000. PAST DUE! PLEASE REMIT!"

"This is all wrong, Daddy!" Cam exclaimed. "I told Doc that I was paying for Galahad's treatment, not you, and he gave me his bill back in August. Doc knew I couldn't pay it all at once, so like I told you and Mom, he said I could work out an installment plan with his receptionist, and that's what I did. I've already made two monthly payments, so the amount's wrong, too! It *was* a thousand dollars, but now it's nine hundred fifty."

"Nine hundred fifty," her father repeated. "So that means you're paying twenty-five dollars a month."

"Yes. Mrs. Grayson said it was okay, so it must have been okay with Doc, too. Please don't worry about it, Daddy," Cam pleaded. "This isn't your debt, it's mine. I'll call Mrs. Grayson tomorrow and straighten everything out!"

"That won't be necessary," Mr. Porter said. "When I

116

opened the envelope this morning, I was sure there had been some mistake, so I called the clinic myself and spoke to a Miss Hunter. She explained that Mrs. Grayson quit a week ago and went to Florida for a long vacation – apparently the computer was too much for her. Since she couldn't figure out how to enter the payments Doc's clients made in the proper files, she just jotted down the amounts on little notes and squirreled them away somewhere, forgetting to tell anyone what she'd done."

Cam groaned. "That sounds like Mrs. Grayson, all right!"

"Naturally, Miss Hunter didn't know anything about it, so she sent out the bills based on the information she found on the computer," her father went on. "I gather the phone's been ringing off the hook with irate animal owners calling to complain. Did Mrs. Grayson happen to give you receipts for the payments you made, Cam? If she did, I'll call Miss Hunter again in the morning so she can bring her files up to date."

"Oh, yes! I have them upstairs in my desk, along with the bill of sale for Galahad. Actually, they're just more little notes, but they show that I paid. And I'm going to pay off the rest, too," Cam promised.

Mr. Porter shook his head. "No, Cam. I can't let you do that, and not just for your own sake. Doc runs a business, not a charitable organization. I also consider him a family friend. He did a fine job on that horse, and it's not fair to make him wait years to be paid in full. I don't know where the money will come from, but I'll have to find it somehow."

"But, Daddy, Doc said it was okay!" Cam cried. "He said he didn't expect me to pay it all at once!" She stuck her hand into her pocket and took out the bills Mr. Cantwell had given her. "This is for part of Galahad's other expenses. I've got fifteen more in my room ..."

117

"And what about the next feed bill? Suppose Galahad needs another visit from the vet, or casts a shoe? I think it's time to face facts," her father said. "This horse of yours has turned into a major liability, one we simply can't afford. I'm sorry, Cam, but I think it's time for Galahad to go."

TEN

CAM STARED AT HER FATHER, HARDLY ABLE TO believe what she had heard. "Oh, no, Daddy!" she cried. "Please don't make me give him up! I'll figure out a way to get a real job, not just baby-sitting when Nat can't. I'm sure there's something I could do – I haven't looked hard enough. Maybe they'd hire me at Stonyfield, where Lacey and I took riding lessons. I know so much more about horses now than I did then! If I worked there after school and on weekends –"

Her mother had come into the room while Cam was speaking, and now she put an arm around Cam's shoulders. "Honey, we can't let you do that," she said. "It's bad enough that Bonnie, Scott, Natalie and Nathan have to work. But you're only fourteen. Daddy and I want you to concentrate on your classes and have some time to have fun the way your older brothers and sisters did at your age. This lean spell we're going through won't last forever, you know. Perhaps next year, or the year after that ..."

"I know how much you've come to love that horse, and how hard you've worked to make him the fine, strong animal he is," Cam's father said. "Believe me, I wish there was some way we could afford to keep him, but there just isn't. Even before Doc's bill arrived, your mother and I were considering selling off some of the acres up by the dunes."

Remembering her dream, Cam gasped. "Oh, no, Daddy! You mustn't! You said you'd never do that!"

"I know I did. I suppose our ancestors will be spinning in their graves, but under the circumstances, I don't have much choice. Both Bonnie and Scott will be in college next year, and even if they apply for financial aid, there are still additional expenses we'll have to cover, not only for them but for the rest of you. Family comes first, Cam. Never forget that."

Blinking back hot tears, Cam swallowed the protests that sprang to her lips. She knew that nothing she could say would make any difference. What her father said was true. Family came first, and if he was prepared to sell some of the beloved land for their sake, she had no right to whine about giving up her horse. She would have to sell Galahad and turn the money over to her parents to help pay off her debts.

"Maybe the people at Stonyfield would buy Galahad," she managed to say around the lump in her throat. "They could use him for riding lessons, and I know they'd take good care of him. I could even visit him sometimes ..."

"You're going to sell Galahad?"

None of them had noticed Ruthie standing in the doorway, and now she ran over to Cam, looking up at her with wide, incredulous eyes. "Why? Don't you love him anymore?"

"I love him a whole lot, Ruthie," she said. "I don't think I knew how much I loved him until right now!"

"So why do you want to sell him, then?"

"Your sister doesn't want to sell him," Mrs. Porter said. "Neither do Daddy or I. The problem is that he's too expensive to keep."

Ruthie frowned. "That's silly, Mom. How can Galahad be too expensive? He only cost two cents!"

"Never mind," Mr. Porter sighed. "Let's just say that Galahad was an experiment that didn't work out."

"I think that stinks!" Ruthie cried, stamping her foot. "You and Mom are being mean and horrid about Galahad, and you're being mean to Cam, too!"

"No, they're not," Cam said sadly. "Try to understand, Ruthie. I wanted to pay for everything Galahad needed, but I couldn't, and I can't keep asking Daddy and Mom to pay his bills when they have so many other expenses. I'll just have to try to find him a new home where he'll be well taken care of."

"Your idea about Stonyfield is a good one, honey," her father said. "Maybe you could ride Galahad over there one day soon and let the owners take a look at him. Meanwhile, I'll contact the local papers and place an ad." Glancing at his watch, he stood up. "I didn't realize it was so late. Let's have dinner."

Mrs. Porter nodded. "Everything's ready. I thought we'd eat in the kitchen tonight," she said. "There's just the four of us – Nat's still out with Jason, and the boys and Bonnie are at work."

While Cam set the table, Ruthie fed the cats. Nobody said a word as they passed around the dishes and served themselves, and no one ate much of Mrs. Porter's delicious stew. Ruthie sulked, picking out the turnips and setting them aside, but her parents didn't scold her or remind her of the starving children in Africa the way they usually did.

Cam felt as though there were a giant rock in the middle of her stomach. After forcing down a few mouthfuls, she finally gave up.

"Sorry, Mom," she mumbled. "I guess I'm not as hungry as I thought I was. May I be excused? I have to give Galahad his evening feed. I'll help Ruthie do the dishes when I come back." The dishwasher had broken down a week ago, and since there was no money to have it repaired everybody took turns washing the dishes.

"Run along, honey," her father said. "Your mother and I are on dish detail tonight."

"Can I come too? I want to say goodbye to Galahad," Ruthie said mournfully.

"Sure," Cam tried to smile. "But you don't have to say goodbye to him yet. He's not going anywhere right away. It may take a while to find someone who wants to buy him."

"I hope it takes forever!" Ruthie muttered.

After Cam got a few carrots from the refrigerator, the girls put on their jackets and went out into the cold, clear night. A million stars twinkled overhead, but Cam was sunk too deep in her own sorrowful thoughts to point out her favorite constellations to Ruthie the way she often did. As they walked in silence across the yard in the direction of the barn, Sailor came out of his doghouse and frisked along beside them, wagging his tail, but Cam and Ruthie didn't even notice him.

Finally Ruthie spoke. "I just had an idea, Cam! If I gave you my allowance every week, could you keep Galahad?"

"Thanks, Ruthie. That's awfully nice of you, but I'm afraid it wouldn't do any good," Cam said. "Mom was right when she said he was too expensive to keep. Nat said pretty much the same thing the other night – she said Galahad's a luxury. I didn't want to believe her, but now I know it's true."

When they reached the barn, the girls entered by a small side door and Cam fumbled for the light switch. Galahad had heard them coming. Even before the light went on, he whickered a welcome, stretching out his neck over the stall door and pricking up his ears. Sailor trotted over to him and stood up on his hind legs, trying to lick the gelding's nose.

"Sailor's going to miss Galahad, too," Ruthie said, "but not as much as I will." Digging into one of the pockets of Cam's jacket, she pulled out a carrot and offered it to the horse.

While Galahad munched on the carrot, Cam put her arms around his neck, resting her cheek against its silky warmth. "It doesn't seem possible that I've had you less than four months," she whispered. "When I first got you, I didn't like you at all. I couldn't wait to sell you. But now that I love everything about you, even your walleye, I *have* to sell you. I know it's necessary, but it just doesn't seem fair!"

The tears Cam had been fighting for so long suddenly overflowed. As she wept, she felt Ruthie's arm slip around her waist.

"Please don't cry, Cam," Ruthie begged, "or else you'll make me cry too, and I hate to cry because my nose gets stuffed up and then I can't breathe! Besides, you're getting Galahad all wet."

With a shaky laugh, Cam let go of the horse and wiped her eyes with her jacket sleeve. "Sorry about that, boy," she said, giving him a gentle pat. Galahad nuzzled her tearstained cheek affectionately, then began snuffling at her pockets.

Ruthie giggled. "Look – he's playing our game."

It didn't take Galahad long to find the rest of the carrots. Cam and Ruthie gave them to him one by one. Then Ruthie poured grain into his feed box while Cam forked hay into the rack above it. After she had filled the gelding's bucket with fresh water, Cam leaned on the stall door watching him eat.

"If only feed and vitamins didn't cost so much," she said with a sigh. "Galahad might as well be eating dollar bills!"

"What if you put him on a diet?" Ruthie suggested hopefully. "If he ate less, you wouldn't have to spend nearly as much."

"I'd never do that, Ruthie," Cam said, shaking her head, "not even to save money. Horses need proper nutrition to stay strong and healthy, and it's especially important for Galahad after the hard life he led before I got him. I'd rather sell him than starve him! Whoever buys him will have to promise to feed him the way Doc said, and give him treats, and be kind to him, and ..."

Cam broke off because she was getting all choked up again. When she was able to speak, she said, "Come on, Ruthie. We'd better go back to the house. I've got homework to do, and I bet you do, too." She gave Galahad one last hug. "See you in the morning," she told the horse. "And after school, we'll go for a ride with Lacey and Speckles. I want to make the most of the time we have left."

Ruthie patted the gelding's nose. "Night, Galahad," she said softly. "Sweet dreams."

As they left the barn, even Sailor seemed dejected.

"Speckles will be awfully sad when Galahad goes away," Ruthie said. "He's her best friend. When are you going to tell Lacey?"

Cam shrugged. "I don't know. Tonight, I guess. I don't really feel like breaking the bad news on the phone, but maybe Lacey knows some nice person who might want to buy him."

"Boy, this really stinks," Ruthie mumbled. "Now you'll have to give up the Centaurs, and Galahad won't get to be Rudolph in the Santa Claus Parade."

"You know, it's kind of funny," Cam said with a rueful smile. "I hadn't thought about that until just now, even though joining the Centaurs was the main reason I bought Galahad from Mr. Barnett in the first place. Remember what he looked like then?"

"Plug-ugly," her sister said promptly. "But now he's plumb beautiful!"

Shaking her head, Cam said, "No, Ruthie, he's really not. We think he's beautiful because we love him. I guess that's what they mean when they say beauty is in the eye of the beholder."

"What's a beholder?"

"Somebody who looks at something."

Ruthie thought about that for a moment. "I don't get it," she said at last. "What about that picture of Moonracer you loaned me? He's beautiful whether anybody's looking at him or not."

"Yes, but Moonracer's just some artist's idea of a perfect horse. He used to be mine, too. I kept comparing Galahad to him, but that wasn't fair, because Galahad's a real live horse and Moonracer is only a dream."

"When Galahad's gone, you can have him back – the picture, I mean," Ruthie offered.

"That's okay, Ruthie. You keep Moonracer."

"Really? For always?"

"For always," Cam tried to smile. "It took a long time, but I've finally outgrown him."

The sisters found their mother putting away the dishes when they came in through the kitchen door. Mrs. Porter told Cam that Lacey had called a few minutes earlier to say she wouldn't be in school the next day. She wouldn't be riding with Cam tomorrow either. Lacey had a fever and a sore throat and was going right to bed, so she didn't want Cam to call her back tonight.

That was fine with Cam. Although she was sorry Lacey was sick, she was also glad to be able to put off telling her about Galahad. Maybe if she didn't talk about it to anyone, it wouldn't seem quite so real.

At school the next morning, Cam wandered from class to class in a fog, unable to concentrate on any of her subjects. In French, Ms. Taggart sprang a surprise quiz on irregular verbs that Cam was pretty sure she flunked. At lunch, she managed to avoid Carla, Marjorie, and Diane by sitting at a table in the far corner of the cafeteria and burying her nose in a book while she tried to choke down her sandwich. The last thing Cam needed was to hear the other girls talking about their horses, or the next Centaurs' trail ride. It was scheduled for a week from Saturday, and by then Galahad might very well be gone.

But while he was still hers Cam wanted to spend as much time as possible with her horse, and although she usually enjoyed her classes, today she resented every minute that kept her from him. Cam had never known a day to drag by so slowly. She was sure all the classroom clocks must be broken.

At long last, however, the final bell rang, and Cam dashed to her locker. She tossed the books she would need for homework into her backpack, grabbed her jacket, and raced for the bus. She'd call Lacey tonight. Then tomorrow she would take Galahad to Stonyfield. If they didn't want him, next week, when the ad appeared in the papers she'd probably have to start showing him to other potential buyers. But for what was left of this beautiful October afternoon, Cam was determined to put all that out of her mind. She and Galahad were going for a nice long ride, just the two of them, as if nothing would ever change.

"Anybody home?" Cam called as she walked through the farmhouse door a short while later.

Nobody answered. Jupiter, Pluto, and Saturn followed her to her room, meowing impatiently while she exchanged her sneakers for her riding boots, then trotted back downstairs with her. When Cam went to the kitchen to get milk for them and an apple for Galahad, she found a note her mother had left for her on the refrigerator door.

Cam dear,
I'm taking off to deliver some pastries to the Maidstone Inn, then will try to drum up some more bakery business at a couple of other restaurants – back around five. Your father and Nate are taking a load of pumpkins and squash to the supermarkets. Ruthie's spending the afternoon at the Fergusons' and sleeping over.
Love you lots,
Mom
P.S.
Daddy called Doc's clinic and told his new receptionist about the payments you made, so at least that part of it is settled.
P.P.S.
Please take one of the containers of spaghetti sauce out of the freezer or we won't have any supper tonight.
P.P.P.S.
The two cupcakes on the counter are for you and Galahad – they're carrot cake, so he ought to love them!

Cam smiled a little, grateful for her mother's effort to cheer her up. She took out the spaghetti sauce and set it on the counter to defrost, poured milk into the cats' bowls, and tucked an apple and the cupcakes into her jacket pockets. Then she scribbled a note of her own:

Taking Galahad for a ride – see you later. Thanks for the cupcakes!
Love you lots too,
C.

Cam let herself out the back door and hurried to the barn. After giving Galahad both cupcakes, the apple, and a lot of hugs, she groomed him until he shone, saddled him, and led him out of the barn.

"I hope you don't mind that it's just you and me today," she said to the gelding as she swung into the saddle. "Lacey's sick, so she and Speckles won't be coming. But if she's better by tomorrow, maybe we can all ride together sometime this weekend." Cam sighed. "We may not be able to do that much longer."

No! I'm not going to worry about that now, she told herself firmly, giving the horse a gentle nudge with her heels. *Just for a couple of hours, I'm going to pretend that nothing's wrong, and that Galahad and I will always be together.*

The gelding needed no urging to pick up his pace. Cam hadn't ridden him since Wednesday, and he was feeling his oats. Neck arched and ears pricked forward, Galahad broke into a brisk trot that quickly carried Cam past the cornfield and vegetable gardens, where nothing flourished now except bright-orange pumpkins, gourds, and winter squash.

Soon it would be Halloween. Cam wondered if Bonnie would have time to decorate the front porch now that she had a job. She usually flanked the front décor with arrangements of corn shocks, pumpkins, and gourds, and each year she made a wonderful pumpkin-headed scarecrow that sat on a chair next to the jack-o'-lantern Cam and Ruthie carved. People driving by the farmhouse would often slow down or even stop to admire the display.

If Bonnie can't do it, maybe I could give it a try, Cam thought. *I don't have her artistic talent, but I'll have a lot of time on my hands once Galahad's gone ...*

To keep herself from brooding about the future, she urged her horse into a canter, heading for the ocean. Maybe a good gallop along the beach would clear the cobwebs from her head and ease the ache in her heart.

ELEVEN

THE LATE-AFTERNOON SUN WAS LOW IN THE SKY when Cam and Galahad started back to the farm. Galahad was no longer wary of the waves or the pounding surf, and they had galloped for miles along the shoreline, filling their lungs with sweet salt air. It was so cool that Galahad wasn't lathered at all. Everything had been as Cam had once imagined it would be with Moonracer, only both better and worse – better because Galahad wasn't a dream, and worse because their days together were numbered.

As they ambled slowly down Skunk Hollow Road, Cam knew she couldn't pretend anymore. She had promised herself that she would take her horse to Stonyfield tomorrow, and that's what she would do. For her family's sake, she had to find a buyer for Galahad a soon as possible.

Lost in her sorrowful thoughts, Cam didn't notice the blue pickup until it suddenly swerved yards ahead of her down the road with its taillights flashing. She was sure she had never seen the truck before, but when the driver got out, she recognized him instantly in spite of the baseball cap covering his bald dome. It was Sam Barnett, and as Cam and Galahad came up to him his ruddy face split in a wide grin.

"Well, I never! It is ol' Plug! What do you know about that!"

He reached out a hand to the gelding, but Galahad flattened his ears and bared his teeth. If Cam hadn't pulled back sharply on the reins, the horse would have nipped him. It was clear to her that Galahad remembered his former owner and the memory wasn't a happy one.

Mr. Barnett just kept on grinning. "Yep, that's Plug all right," he said. "When I passed you, I said to myself, 'That horse looks a heck of a lot like Spunky used to before he got plug-ugly,' so I pulled over to take a closer look. You did a real good job on him, kid, even if he's still mean as sin."

"Thank you, Mr. Barnett," Cam said stiffly. "He's not really mean, though. Galahad never acts that way anymore – or he didn't until just now."

"Oh, yeah? Well, guess I'll have to take your word for it." The farmer scratched his head. "What did you call him just now?"

"His new name is Galahad."

Mr. Barnett roared with laughter, startling the gelding, who threw up his head and snorted. "Galahad! That's a good one, that is! I never heard of naming an animal after a tractor before!"

Cam would have mentioned King Arthur's Round Table, but since she really had taken Galahad's name from a tractor ad, she didn't. Instead, she said, politely but not truthfully, "Well, it's been nice seeing you again, Mr. Barnett. We have to be getting home now ..."

"Take it easy, sis. What's your hurry? I want to take a gander at this fella."

The farmer walked around Galahad, eyeing him from nose to tail and keeping well out of range of the horse's fidgety hind hooves. When he had completed his inspection, he folded his arms and leaned against the back of his truck, a thoughtful expression on his face.

"Like I said before, you did a real good job. This horse has to be worth plenty more than you paid me for him. What was it – ten cents?"

"Two," Cam mumbled.

"Huh? Speak up, sis. I didn't hear you."

She raised her voice. "*Two cents*. You said for two cents you'd give him away, and that's what I paid you for him. I made out a bill of sale and you signed it."

"Oh, yeah, I remember now. Guess that wasn't the smartest deal I ever made, considering that I threw in his saddle and bridle for nothing ..."

Cam tightened her grip on Galahad's reins. A cold chill ran down her spine. What was Mr. Barnett leading up to?

"Suppose I was to offer you twenty bucks to buy him back?" he said. "That'd be a pretty good return on your investment, now wouldn't it? I got twenty bucks right here in my pocket."

"No!" Cam cried. Even if he had offered a hundred times that amount, her reaction would have been the same.

Mr. Barnett rubbed his chin. "Well now, suppose something else. Suppose that bill of sale I signed isn't worth the paper it's written on because you're underage? For all we know, Plug-Ugly might still be mine and I'd have the right to take him back and auction him off to the highest bidder."

The chill penetrated to Cam's very bones. The only way she was able to bear the thought of selling Galahad was the knowledge that the money would help pay off her debt to her father and to Doc. Cam also intended to make very sure that whoever bought her horse would give him the loving care he deserved. But if Sam Barnett reclaimed him, she'd lose everything.

"You wouldn't, would you?" she cried.

"Maybe I would, and maybe I wouldn't. It all depends."

"On what?"

Instead of answering her question, the farmer said, "Tell me something, sis. Now that you've had ol' what's-his-name for a while, how do you feel about him?"

"Oh, Mr. Barnett, I love him!" Cam said fervently. "Galahad's the best horse in the whole world!"

He nodded. "My daughter Mandy thought so too, back when he was Spunky. 'Worth his weight in gold,' she used to say ..."

After one more long, appraising look at Galahad, Mr. Barnett said, "Well, time I was moving along. Can't keep the cows waiting when they're ready to be milked."

He climbed into the cab of his truck, revved up the engine, and drove off without another word, but Cam was sure she hadn't seen the last of Sam Barnett.

As she walked Galahad down the road, a tight knot of fear formed in her chest. What would she do if he tried to take her horse away? What could she do? Even if Mr. Barnett didn't show up to claim him right away, he might very well see the ads in the papers next week. Would he come banging on the door, insisting that he was the gelding's rightful owner and demanding that when Cam sold Galahad, she turn over the money to him? Could he accuse her of being a horse thief and have her put in jail?

All the way back to the barn, Cam's brain whirled with awful possibilities. By the time she had rubbed Galahad down and given him his evening feed, she had a splitting headache and her throat felt raw.

Maybe I'm coming down with the same thing Lacey's got, Cam thought gloomily. *I wouldn't be surprised. Everything else is going wrong lately!*

On second thought, maybe it wouldn't be so bad after all. If she were *really* sick, she could put off taking Galahad to Stonyfield for a couple of days. Deciding to take her temperature if she didn't feel better in a little while, Cam distracted the gelding from his feed box long enough to give him a kiss on the nose before she left the barn.

Bonnie was at the stove stirring the spaghetti sauce when Cam came into the kitchen. "Have a nice ride?" she asked.

"Sort of," Cam hedged. "Isn't Mom back yet?"

"No – she just phoned to say she's in Montauk talking to some people at a new restaurant that's about to open, but she'll be on her way home soon. She's pretty sure they're going to give her an order to supply all of their baked goods."

"That's great. It's about time we had some good news around here," Cam muttered.

She was on her way out of the room when Bonnie added, "Oh, by the way, you got a bunch of calls while you were out. Some girls named Carla and Megan, and Lacey called twice. They all said it was important, and to call back as soon as you can."

Cam's shoulders slumped. "They've probably changed the date of the next Centaurs meeting or something. I haven't spoken to Lacey since Wednesday, so I guess I'd better call her. I don't feel much like talking to any of them right now, though."

"I can imagine," Bonnie said. "Mom and Dad told me about Galahad last night. I'm really sorry, Cam. I wish it didn't have to be this way."

"Yeah, me too. But you know what Grandma always says – if wishes were horses, beggars would ride."

Bonnie nodded. "She got that right. But she was wrong about something else. Where Galahad is concerned, you *did* make a silk purse out of a sow's ear."

"I did, didn't I?" Cam sighed. "But you know what, Bonnie? Sometimes I almost wish I hadn't!"

She hung her jacket in the hall closet, then went up to her parents' room and flopped down on the bed, staring at the phone. It seemed like yesterday when Cam had called to tell Lacey the wonderful news that she had her very own horse. They had both been so happy and excited! Now she was so miserable that it was a major effort just to pick up the receiver and dial Lacey's number.

A gruff voice answered on the second ring. Thinking it was Mr. Vining, Cam said, "This is Cam Porter. May I please speak to Lacey?"

"You *are* speaking to her," Lacey croaked. "This is me."

"Gee, Lacey, you sound terrible," Cam exclaimed. "How are you feeling?"

"Terrible, and not just because of the cold. Oh, Cam, the most awful thing just happened!"

Lacey had taken the words right out of Cam's mouth. "You bet it has!" she said, surprised. "But how did you –"

Lacey didn't let her continue. "I thought Megan or Carla might have finally reached you. Megan's been calling all the Centaurs. You can come to the emergency meeting, can't you?"

Completely bewildered, Cam said, "What meeting? What's the emergency? What are you talking about?"

"Then you don't know?" Lacey sounded astonished.

"No, Lacey, I do not know. I do not have the faintest idea what's going on. Now, are you going to tell me or what?"

"It's Seabreeze –" Lacey began, but before she could say more she had a coughing fit.

"What about Seabreeze? Oh, Lacey, it hasn't burned down, has it?" Cam cried. A stable fire was one of the worst things she could possibly imagine, even worse than losing Galahad. At least he was alive and well. What if Speckles and the other horses had been badly hurt, or killed?

Lacey had recovered, and now she said, "Not that bad, but almost. It's gone up. *Way* up!"

Cam gasped in horror. "The stable blew up?"

"No! Nothing blew up!" Lacey squawked. "The boarding rates *went* up sky high. Beginning next month, they're going to be *double* what they are now! When my dad got the notice this morning, I'm surprised your parents didn't hear him yelling all the way out at the farm! He and Mom are practically in a state of shock, and so are Carla's folks, and Marjorie's and Diane's."

"Oh, wow!" Cam breathed. "Seabreeze is the only boarding stable in Shorehaven. What are you guys going to do?"

"Look somewhere else, I guess. Mr. Luchese says if Carla can't find a cheaper place to board Gremlin in the next couple of weeks, he'll have to sell him. The rest of the Seabreeze crowd are in the same boat."

"Your parents wouldn't make you give up Speckles, would they?"

"I don't know," Lacey said. She sounded as if she were on the verge of tears. "They might not have any choice."

Cam was stunned. Blinking back her own sympathetic tears, she said, "I can't believe this! I'm all bent out of

136

shape because I have to sell Galahad, and now I find out you and some of the other girls could lose your horses too!"

"Oh, Cam, I'm so sorry!" Lacey sniffled. "I didn't think things could get any worse, but they just did! How come?"

Cam told her the whole story, then said, "There's nothing I can do about Galahad, but if all the Centaurs put their heads together, maybe we can solve your problem. Where do Megan and the other girls from Brightwater board their horses? They might know of some stables that charge a lot less than Seabreeze."

"That's what the emergency meeting's about," Lacey said. "It's tonight, seven thirty, my place again because Mom won't let me go out of the house."

"I'll be there if I have to walk," Cam promised.

At supper when Cam explained to her parents about the Centaurs' troubles and the meeting, they agreed to let her go. Bonnie volunteered to drive her to Lacey's and to pick her up if nobody could bring her home.

"Just give me a call if you need a ride," Bonnie said as she pulled up in front of the Vinings' house a little before seven thirty. "I'll be working on a paper that's due on Monday, so I'll be more than ready to take a break in a few hours."

"It probably won't be necessary, but thanks anyway." Cam struggled with the door of the ancient car until it opened. "Good luck with your paper."

"Good luck with your meeting!"

Bonnie drove away and Cam walked up the flagstone path. When she rang the doorbell, Mrs. Vining let her in. "They're all in the family room," she said, and walked with Cam to the stairs. "I tell you, Cam, Mr. Vining and I are at our wits' end. *Double* the rates! What do those people at Seabreeze think we

137

are – movie stars or millionaires? Maybe somebody like that could afford to pay those prices, but we certainly can't." She heaved a sigh. "Lacey will be heartbroken if she has to give up Speckles, but I guess hardware and horses just don't mix."

Cam couldn't think of anything comforting to say, so she just nodded and said nothing.

When she came down the stairs into the family room, she saw eight glum faces. One of them belonged to Lacey, who was curled up in an armchair in her pajamas and bathrobe. Her nose was red, her eyes were bleary, and she was clutching a box of tissues. Lacey waved to Cam and sneezed. Cam waved back and sat down on the sofa between Brenda and Diane.

"Take a look at this," Diane said grimly, handing her a piece of paper. "It's the letter Seabreeze sent to all their boarders."

Cam glanced at the headline, HOME IS WHERE YOUR HORSE IS, then scanned the letter quickly. It described in glowing terms the renovations and improvements the owners were in the process of making. These included an indoor riding ring, complete with Olympic-style jumps, soda and snack machines and wall-to-wall carpeting in what was called the "social room," and soothing music piped into the stable twenty-four hours a day. Seabreeze Stables would be the finest boarding facility on the whole South Fork "because we want your special horse to enjoy the luxury he/she deserves."

The final paragraph of the letter went on to state that due to all of the above, a "slight" increase in the "modest" boarding fees would take effect in November, and expressed the hope this would not inconvenience any of the stable's valued patrons. The letter ended with a reminder that payment was due on the first of the month.

"This is unreal!" Cam exclaimed when she finished reading. "Canned music? Carpeting in the social room? I'm surprised they're not carpeting the stalls and putting in a swimming pool for the horses!"

"That'll probably come next," Carla muttered.

Megan stood up and walked over to stand in front of the fireplace, facing the group. "Okay, we all know what the problem is," she said. "Seabreeze has priced four of our members right out of the market. So what are we going to do about it?"

Diane sprang up from the sofa. "We could make signs and picket the stable!"

"They wouldn't care about that," Marjorie said. "In fact, they'd probably love the publicity." Diane wilted and sat down again. "We're small potatoes, and they're aiming for people with big bucks. What about you guys from Brightwater? Is there any room where you board your horses?"

"Not where Brenda and I keep Pretty Boy and Hotshot," Erica said. "They're pretty reasonable, but it's a really small stable and they're full up."

"Same here. How about you, Megan? Any room where you keep Stormy?" Tamara asked.

Megan made a face. "Are you kidding? You've seen that place. It's about the size of a chicken coop, and there are two other horses besides Stormy. They have to take turns to breathe!"

"What about Stonyfield?" Cam suggested. "They might board horses there. Has anybody checked it out?"

"My dad did," Carla said. "They don't."

"I guess we could try Bodtauk," Lacey croaked.

Everybody stared at her. "Bod Talk? What's that? Sounds like one of those fitness spas," Marjorie said.

"She means Montauk," Cam translated. "You might find a cheaper place there, but it's awfully far away."

Megan sighed. "There just has to be some way out of this mess. It would be too awful if four of the Centaurs had to give up their horses."

"It sure would," Tamara said. "If only we had a little more time! We won't make much of a showing in the Santa Claus Parade with only five reindeer."

Lacey glanced at Cam, but Cam shook her head. She couldn't bring herself to tell the others that Galahad would most likely be gone by then too.

Marjorie scowled. "It's not fair! Just because Seabreeze is the only stable in town they think they can charge the earth and get away with it."

"Yeah – they say 'home is where your horse is,' but in two weeks *our* horses will be homeless," Diane said bitterly. "We probably won't even be able to find buyers for them by then. What am I supposed to do – tie Lightfoot up in my backyard?"

No one had an answer for her. In the gloomy silence that followed, Cam thought, *Home is where your horse is. That's exactly the way I feel about Galahad. It won't be the same after he's gone. I'll never set foot in the barn again without picturing him sticking his head out over his stall door to greet me. It'll be just a big empty space ...*

Suddenly she sat bolt upright. *A big empty space with a lot of empty stalls!*

But those stalls didn't have to stay empty. How had Cam missed seeing that the solution to her friends' problem and her own had been right under her nose all along? Speckles, Lightfoot, Gremlin, and Dawn could move into the barn! Even if she charged less than the girls' parents had been paying at Seabreeze up to now, there would be enough money coming in each month to cover Galahad's expenses with plenty left over. Lacey, Carla, Marjorie, Diane, and Cam could all keep their horses, and Cam could help her family at the same time!

With a gleeful whoop, Cam leaped to her feet. Beaming at her startled friends, she shouted, "Guess what, everybody? I just had the most fantastic idea!"

TWELVE

THE CENTAURS WERE THRILLED WITH CAM'S plan, and so were Mr. and Mrs. Vining. Of course, nothing could be settled until Cam had gotten her parents' approval, but she was determined to talk to them about it that very night. Mr. Vining was so enthusiastic that when he drove Cam home, he offered to come in and discuss the business angle of her project with her mother and father.

Hal and Ruth-Ann Porter were watching television in the living room when Cam and Lacey's father arrived. They were surprised to see him, and they were even more surprised when Cam blurted out her wonderful idea, which Mr. Vining heartily endorsed. Her parents weren't as excited as Cam had hoped they would be, but to her great relief, they didn't immediately reject her plan either.

The four of them went into the kitchen, where Mrs. Porter made coffee and brought out more carrot cupcakes. Then they sat around the kitchen table talking about the pros and cons of starting a boarding business. Although Cam didn't have much to add to the conversation, she listened closely to every word Mr. Vining and her parents said, amazed at how complicated it all sounded. Everything had seemed so simple to her – after they got rid of the junk cluttering up the empty stalls, put clean straw on the floor, and provided feed and water, the horses would move right in.

But there was insurance to consider and town regulations to look into. Mr. Vining said he would find out if Cam's father would need some kind of permit, which seemed pretty silly to her. Why should he need a permit just because he would be stabling five horses instead of one? The one thing that Cam had feared might be a problem was the expense of feeding those five horses, but her father said if he bought in large quantities from a discount distributor he knew of up-island, it wouldn't cost much at all.

Mr. Vining suggested a boarding fee that he considered reasonable, and when Mr. and Mrs. Porter agreed that it was, he promised to call the Lucheses, the Steinbergs, and the Ralstons first thing in the morning.

"If none of them object, and I see no reason why they should, then it's full speed ahead," he said as they all rose from the table. "I don't mind telling you, this is a huge load off my mind, not to mention my wallet! I'm sure my blood pressure went up ten points when I got that letter from Seabreeze. The last thing I wanted to do was sell Lacey's mare, but I didn't see any way around it until Cam saved the day."

"It was the only way I could think of for all of us to keep our horses, Mr. Vining," Cam said. "I almost had to give up Galahad, too, and if that had happened –" She shivered. "I just don't want to think about it." Then she grinned. "Wait till Ruthie hears! She'll hit the ceiling! If it wasn't so late, I'd call her at the Fergusons' right now."

After Mrs. Porter wrapped some cupcakes for Mr. Vining to take home to Lacey and her mother, Cam and her father walked him to the front door. The two men shook hands, and when Mr. Vining had left, Cam's father smiled at her.

"Well, young lady, it looks like we're in the boarding business."

Cam gave him a gigantic hug. "Thank you, Daddy," she murmured.

"No, honey. Thank you," Mr. Porter said, resting his cheek on the top of her tousled blond head. "Your idea got a lot of people out of a very tight spot. I'm proud of you."

Coming into the hall, Cam's mother put her arms around them both. "So am I," she said. "I'm also pooped, and it's almost eleven o'clock. We have a busy time ahead of us getting ready for our paying guests, so we'd better rest up while we can."

Cam realized that she was exhausted too, but before she went to bed there was one very important thing she had to do.

"Back in a minute," she said, racing out the front door. As she ran toward the barn her heart was singing. Galahad was hers to keep, and she couldn't wait to tell him so.

When she ran inside and turned on the light, the gelding made his usual welcoming noises. Instead of rushing straight to him, however, Cam paused, looking around the vast, dim space. The other stalls were filled with junk and cobwebs now, but they wouldn't be for long. In her mind's eye, Cam could clearly see Speckles in the one next to Galahad. In the stall on the other side of Speckles was Carla's bay gelding, Gremlin ...

Or maybe not, she thought, frowning. *Maybe Speckles would like to have another mare for a neighbor. Okay, then I'll put Lightfoot there, and Dawn and Gremlin can have the two stalls across from them – unless Marjorie and Carla have other ideas, of course. Whatever they want to do will be fine with me!*

144

Galahad whuffled impatiently and pawed the floor, bringing Cam back to the present. She ran to him and threw her arms around his neck.

"Everything's going to be all right," she told the gelding. "You're mine forever and ever! Nobody can take you away from me now. And wait till you meet your new roommates! You'll never be lonely again, Galahad. That's a promise."

Over the next two weeks everybody pitched in to prepare the barn for its new occupants. After school and on weekends all the Centaurs took turns helping Cam and her family clean out the stalls and get rid of all the odds and ends that had accumulated there over the years. Tamara's father came out to the farm one Saturday and installed new, brighter lights in the barn free of charge. Mr. Vining contributed new hinges and latches for the stall doors that needed them, and Mr. Porter and Scott replaced several rotting floorboards. They all worked very hard and Cam worked hardest of all, but since it was a labor of love, she enjoyed every minute of it.

Next to Cam, Ruthie was the happiest of all. "I told all my friends that my sister's gonna have five horses!" she announced one night at supper near the end of October. "Boy, were they ever jealous!"

"Well, four of those horses don't belong to Cam, you know," Natalie reminded her. "Galahad's the only one who's really hers."

"Yeah, but they don't know that," Ruthie said cheerfully. "Anyway, he's the *best* one. I'm so glad he's gonna be Rudolph in the Santa Claus Parade."

"I thought I'd start working with you guys on the antlers and wreaths in a couple of weeks," Bonnie said to Cam.

145

"Now that I've done the Halloween decorations for the porch, I'll have some free time."

"That'll be great," Cam said. "Did I tell all of you that Tamara Benning's dad is going to make Galahad a light-up nose? It'll be attached to the noseband of his bridle and run on batteries."

"Hey, remember that old Robert Redford movie we saw on TV last week, *The Electric Horseman*? Meet Cam Porter, the Electric Horsewoman!" Nathan teased.

By the first week in November, all the work on the barn had been done. On a blustery, overcast Saturday afternoon, Lacey, Marjorie, Carla, and Diane rode their horses to their new home. The night before, Cam, Natalie, and Ruthie had tied big red bows to all the stall doors, including Galahad's, and Bonnie had lettered, "WELCOME, CENTAURS!" on an old sheet that Scott nailed to the front of the barn.

Grinning from ear to ear, Cam met her friends at the door and led them inside, where they were greeted by Galahad's excited whickering and soft rock music from Nathan's transistor radio.

"All the luxuries your special horses deserve! What does Seabreeze have that we haven't got?" she joked. "I have to admit we don't have a social room yet, but as soon as your horses are settled in, Mom's invited everybody to the house for a celebration – hot spiced cider, homemade doughnuts, and apple cake."

"This is so neat," Lacey said as she and the others dismounted and led their horses to the stalls they had selected earlier in the week. "It's almost too good to be true!"

"I bet Galahad feels the same way," Cam said, stroking

the gelding's neck. "I promised him he'd never be lonely again, but I don't think he believed me until now."

Ruthie came running into the barn carrying a basket full of shiny red apples. "These are welcome-home treats," she announced, handing an apple to each girl. "For the *horses*, not you!" she added as Lacey pretended to bite into hers.

When the horses had all been given their treats, Ruthie said, "Mom says to hurry up – the cider's getting cold."

"Come on, guys," Diane said. "I don't know about the rest of you, but I'm freezing to death, and hot cider's going to taste awfully good."

The others trooped out of the barn, but Cam lingered behind.

"Aren't you coming, Cam?" Lacey called.

"You go ahead. I'll be there in a minute."

When all the girls had left, Cam gazed from one stall to another, a contented smile on her face. It was exactly as she had imagined it on the night she had first come up with her plan. There they all were – Dawn, Lightfoot, Gremlin, Speckles, and most important of all, Galahad.

I guess sometimes wishes really do come true, she thought. Giving Galahad a loving pat, Cam headed for the door.

Then she stopped in her tracks.

A blue pickup truck was just pulling up in front of the barn. Behind the wheel was Sam Barnett, and a woman was sitting next to him.

For a moment, Cam couldn't breathe. Her heart was pounding so hard she thought she might pass out. The wonderful, exciting events of the past few weeks had driven the memory of her last encounter with Mr. Barnett right out of her head. Now it all came rushing back. The farmer's exact words echoed in her brain: "Plug-Ugly might still be mine, and I'd have the right to take him back and auction him off to the highest bidder."

And here he was, with a potential buyer!

Cam couldn't let him take her horse away, not after everything she'd done to keep him! Her first frantic impulse was to leap on Galahad's bare back and gallop him out of the barn, putting as much distance as possible between him and his former owner. But even as she was racing to the gelding's stall, Mr. Barnett got out of the truck and marched up to the door.

"That you, sis?" he called, peering inside.

Trapped!

"Yes – it's me," Cam replied in a voice that quivered. Squaring her shoulders, she stood in front of Galahad's stall. If Mr. Barnett meant to take him away, he'd have to knock her down first!

As the farmer strolled into the barn, he looked around with interest. "Well, well, well," he said. "Looks like Plug's got plenty of company. Don't tell me you bought all these horses for two cents each."

Cam's mouth was so dry she could hardly speak. "They're – they're not mine," she managed to say. "We're just boarding them. They belong to the members of a riding club called the South Shore Centaurs."

"That explains the sign, then. Listen, kid, how about bringing ol' Plug outside? I got somebody with me who wants to take a look at him."

Gathering all her courage, Cam cried, "No! I won't do it! You have no right to sell him. He's my horse – I bought him from you fair and square! You can take me to court or throw me in jail, but I won't give Galahad up!"

Mr. Barnett stared at her. "Hey, now just hang on a minute!" he said loudly. "Who said anything about –"

148

A woman's voice cut him off. "What's all the shouting about? I thought you said I could see Spunky."

As she walked toward them, Cam saw that the woman was young and pretty, with long auburn hair. She was wearing a bright red parka, and her cheeks were pink from the cold.

"I'm sorry, miss, but this horse belongs to me, and he's not for sale," Cam said, folding her arms across her chest.

The young woman laughed. "I know that. Dad told me all about it."

Cam blinked. "Dad? Mr. Barnett is your father?"

"That's right. I'm Mandy Barnett. I've been looking forward to meeting you, Cam. When Dad told me he'd sold Spunky, I was pretty upset, but after he described what a couple of years out to pasture had done to my poor horse, I decided it was probably for the best. My husband and I are visiting my folks for a few days, and when Dad offered to bring me out here to say hello to Spunky, I jumped at the chance."

Mandy stepped around Cam and gazed at Galahad for a long moment, then put her arms around the gelding's neck, resting her cheek against it as Cam so often did. When she released him, Mandy said, "He looks absolutely wonderful, Cam. Dad said my horse couldn't have found a better home, and he's obviously right."

Cam stared at Mr. Barnett in astonishment. "But – but two weeks ago you threatened to take Galahad back and sell him!"

The farmer held up one hand. "Now hold it right there, sis. I didn't do nothing of the kind! I said *supposing* I took him back. Supposing ain't the same thing as threatening, now is it?"

"Well, no, but ..."

"You're darned right it ain't!" Mr. Barnett blustered. "Oh, I gotta admit the thought crossed my mind, but when you said you loved that horse, you kinda reminded me of Mandy here when she was a kid. She'd've cried her eyes out if anybody took him away from her then, and I sure didn't want to make some other kid cry."

"By the way, I understand you've given Spunky a new name," Mandy said. "Galahad, like the knight of King Arthur's Round Table."

Speechless and limp with relief, Cam could only nod, but Mr. Barnett bellowed, "What do you mean, knight? She didn't name him after no knight. She named him after a tractor!"

Cam's and Mandy's eyes met, and they grinned at each other.

Mr. Barnett looked at them suspiciously. "What's so funny?"

Mandy winked at Cam. "Nothing, Dad," she said, linking her arm through his. "We'd better be going now. I'm sure Cam has better things to do than stand around talking to us."

"Yes, I do!" Cam blurted. Then, realizing how rude that sounded, she blushed. "Sorry – what I mean is, some of the Centaurs are having kind of a party at my house, and I'd like it very much if you'd both come."

"Well, now, I don't know ..." Mr. Barnett mumbled, but Mandy tugged on his arm.

"Oh, come on, Dad. Don't be an old stick-in-the mud. I love parties, and I'd like to hear about this riding club Cam belongs to. That's just the kind of thing I'd have loved when I was her age."

Cam beamed at them both. "Terrific! This will be one celebration I'll never, ever forget!"

On the Saturday after Thanksgiving, both sides of Shorehaven's Main Street were crowded with men, women, and children, all cheering, clapping their gloved hands, and waving to their friends and relatives who were marching in the Santa Claus parade. They applauded the Shorehaven High School Band, the Bagpipers, the brightly costumed Cub Scouts and Brownies, the Veterans of Foreign Wars, the peewee soccer teams, and the various lavishly decorated floats.

But the loudest cheers and the most enthusiastic applause came at the very end. Leading the Santa Claus float were eight smiling girls dressed up as Santa's elves in red and green. They were riding two by two on high-stepping horses with reindeer antlers on their heads and wreaths tied with bright red bows around their necks.

Out in front all by herself was the happiest girl on Long Island's whole South Fork, riding a gleaming chestnut gelding. Like the other horses, he was wearing antlers and a wreath, but a bright red electric bulb attached to his noseband blinked on and off as he pranced along.

Cam held her head high, beaming proudly as she waved to the crowd from Galahad's back. *If I were any happier, I'd probably explode into a million pieces!* She thought. *Talk about a dream come true!*

Cam grinned so broadly that she felt her cold face might crack. She spotted her entire family standing on the sidelines. They had all turned out to see Galahad's shining moment. Ruthie jumped up and down, waving wildly as Cam and the rest of the Centaurs passed. Cam waved back happily.

"Galahad's the most beautiful horse in the whole wide world!" Ruthie shouted. "He's even beautifuller than Moonracer!"

"You're right, Ruthie," Cam shouted back. "He is!"